Hawk

SAMUEL'S PRIDE SERIES BOOK 6

KATHI S. BARTON

This is a work of fiction. Names, characters, places, and incidents are products of the author's imagination or are used fictitiously and are not to be construed as real. Any resemblance to actual events, locations, organizations, or person, living or dead, is entirely coincidental.

World Castle Publishing, LLC
Pensacola, Florida
Copyright © Kathi S. Barton 2015
Hardback ISBN: 9781629893372
Print ISBN: 9781629893389
eBook ISBN: 9781629893396
First Edition World Castle Publishing, LLC, September 21, 2015
http://www.worldcastlepublishing.com

Licensing Notes

Cover: Karen Fuller
Editor: Eric Johnston
Editor: Maxine Bringenberg

CHAPTER 1

Awnia moved among the crowds of people without raising her head. She watched feet as they hurried to get around her and to wherever they were going. Everyone was always in such a hurry any more. Avoiding everyone, especially their touch, had always been a priority to her, and today was no different. So when someone touched her elbow and jerked her around, she knew everything about the man in just that instant...more than likely a great deal more than he knew about himself.

"Take this." She backed away from the blue zippered bag that he'd shoved at her. "Here is your part, take it."

"I don't know you." Which in truth was a lie, but she took another step back. "I have no idea what you're talking about. And I don't want whatever that is."

It was full of money...several thousand dollars' worth. Awnia had no use for such things, and wondered why, of all the people around her, he'd told her. She couldn't find any other reason for it in his head other than it had to be her she gave the bag to.

"Yes you do. You told me to get it. Now here. Take it." She took another step back when he hit her in the chest with it. She knew he thought she'd pick it up when it hit the sidewalk between them, but she only stared at him. "Pick it up and take it. Now. I don't have a lot of time for this."

Awnia started to turn and walk away. There was no reason for her to do as he was demanding, and if she stood there much longer, the police were going to come and take them both away. And Awnia had no desire to be caught up in things like that. But as soon as she turned away, he grabbed her by the arm again, and the connection between them was complete.

"You need to let me go." He didn't, of course, and she tried to jerk from his grasp. "I'm not going to tell you again to let me go. I don't know you or what you're about. But if you don't release me, I am going to hurt you."

"Take the fucking money. It's all you fucking have to do." Shaking her head, she let a little of herself go and he jerked back from her. "What the fuck?"

The burn to his hand was minor when compared to what she might have done to him. But he picked up the blue bag now and tried to shove it at her once more. Again she backed away, and watched as he reached into the front of his pants and pulled out a gun.

"You can't shoot me." The man grinned at her as he pointed it at her. "If you shoot me, it's going to cause problems with the man you're working for. He said no violence, and if you were caught by the police, he said that he'd leave you there to rot. I think this is what he meant."

"What the fuck do you know? They said if I didn't give it to you as soon as you came outta that building, I was taking the fall for everything. And, sister, I am not taking the fall for you being a bitch." He pointed the gun to her head, and the people around them did nothing but give them a wider berth. "Take the damned money so I can get on with my life."

Awnia didn't want to hurt him, but it was quickly becoming clear that there was no reasoning with him. Putting out her finger, she touched his hand that held the gun. His screams cut through her head like a spike. Before she could move away from him, however, someone grabbed her from behind and told her to stand down. This time when the cool feel of the weapon the person held touched her, she knew it would hurt her.

"I don't know him." The police officer in front of her only nodded as he put cuffs on the man with the gun. The one behind her was careful not to touch her, she noticed, so she was unable to find out what was going on. "I don't have any idea why he picked me, but I don't know him."

The man behind her laughed as he cuffed her as well. The thick touch of his gloves was the first clue she was in bigger trouble than she had first thought. The touch, when he brushed against her with his arm, was so brief she nearly missed it. Now she was afraid. This was not just a routine arrest. This man was no better than the one who had tried to shoot her…maybe even a little worse.

"Sure you don't, honey. We already have things all worked out for the two of you. Just as soon as we get you downtown. We're just gonna write this one up as you pretended this shit to get away. Well, you aren't going anywhere. Not until we take care of a little business here. You might say we're working for the wrong side of the lawman today."

His laughter made her think of braying donkeys. And when he lifted her up, none too gently, she had a feeling that he might be related to them as well. The man was a real ass.

She was shoved into a cruiser a few minutes later. Awnia never said another word after that, not even when they asked her what her full name was. There were others out there that would like that information as well, but as far as she knew, no one but her knew it. The ride to wherever they were going was made mostly with the two officers in the front complaining about someone named Pittsburg, and how he had the attitude of a badger. She tuned them out in favor of contacting her friend, her only friend.

I am in trouble. He asked her when she wasn't. *I've been taken into custody by two men that are police officers, and am currently being taken to the station for a crime I have no idea about. There is a man that came to me about a fictitious crime, and now they are taking me away from anything I know.*

Vinnie laughed again. *You should have zapped them all and been done with it. I know that you have these rules and all, but when you're being taken against your will, it's best to deal with it as quickly as possible.*

Will you come for me? She waited for him to answer her as the car came to a stop. *Vinnie, this is not a station house. I'm at a warehouse. I think I might be in serious trouble here.*

Where? All humor was gone from his voice. *Tell me what you see. Are there any landmarks for you to give me? Damn it all to hell, Awnia, I told you that you had to stop getting into trouble. I love you too much to have you get hurt by some human. Or that asshole.*

Ignoring his comment, she told him what she could see. *A green roof with brick. Many abandoned houses surrounding us, and the building they are in front of has a name faded on the front. Machete something. I'm not sure.* He told her to close her eyes and he'd find her. *There is nothing for you to search with. Other than our ability to speak, we have nothing left. When you mated, we lost our connection. I'm sorry. But I'm very scared right now.*

His cursing made her smile. The dragon could string them together like no one she'd ever met. But when he spoke to her again, she knew that he was going to try his best to find her. Or he'd die trying.

My mate and I are coming to you. Are you still where you were? The same city? She told him no, she was in Erie County, New York. *I'm coming, love. We'll be there soon.*

I do hope so. As she was pulled out of the back of the car, she fell. The officers didn't lift her up or help her to stand, but continued to pull her with them by the cuffs. *Hurry, Vinnie. I think they might know what I am. Neither of them has touched me at all but for a brush, which gave me little information other than the fact that he isn't pleased with having to bring me here.*

Christ, baby, I'm coming.

As Awnia was pulled into the building by her hair now, she said nothing. The cuffs at her wrists prevented her from touching the men, and she thought they knew that as well. As soon as she was tossed into a cage, she had a feeling that no matter how quickly he got there, Vinnie was going to be too late. Closing her eyes, she tried to calm herself before she hurt her captors and herself trying to get away.

"Hello, goddess." The voice behind her had her opening her eyes. She knew it. And him. He was someone from her past that she'd hoped to never encounter again. The Mad Hatter had hurt her badly before. "So you've been working with my friend, Steven, I see."

The young man who had accosted her on the street was jerked in front of her. He grinned at her as he pulled the money from the blue envelope. Steven was stuffing it into his pocket after kissing it when he was shot in the head. Awnia didn't even feel badly for the man. He'd made his bed, and now he was going to be buried in it.

"You know that I did not have a thing to do with him. He is your pawn—your dead pawn—and we both know it."

She didn't turn toward the man but tried to think how to get out of the bonds at her wrist. "You are supposed to be dead. I think the last time we were together, you pissed me off and I hurt you."

"And thanks to you, I was nearly killed." He stepped in front of her, and she could only stare. "You did a bang-up job on making sure that no one would come near me, though, didn't you? Do you have any idea how long it took me to even look like this? You ruined me when you touched me that day. And now, my dear goddess, you're going to make me a very wealthy man."

"I should have killed you." The cuff on her right wrist opened when she heated it up. It was only steel, and the melting point was a good deal less than she could heat up to. Then the other. When she stood up, Hatter, as she had always called him, scrambled back quickly. "This will not happen again, Hatter. I will not help you in any way. I won't let her kill me, and I certainly won't let you take me easily. Not ever. Do you hear me?"

"Oh yes, I can hear you. And so you say about not helping me. I've got you right now, and you're going to do as I say for a change."

The blast hit her in the back. It wasn't a bullet but something powerful, like magic...cold, hard magic. The second time it hit her, she fell forward and put her hands on the bars. They started to heat from her fear and pain. Hatter tried to shove her back by using a piece of wood, of all things, and it caught fire almost immediately. Stupid man didn't know you didn't bring a weapon of wood to a fire fight?

The heat in her hands burned through the bars, and as they melted, her body took its true shape. Hot and molten, she looked at Hatter through the haze of heat. As people screamed, she knew that Hatter had gotten away, but it was too late for her to go for him now. As she soared to the sky, her body in no shape to heal itself, she hoped that Vinnie would find her soon.

~~~

"Come on, baby, talk to me." Hawk ran his hands over the hood of the car and purred to it again. "You know I can't help you if you don't talk to me."

The voice sputtered to life, and he had to smile. The thing was English-made and the voice that told him where she hurt was very British. Hawk knew that soon he'd be able to repair the damage done to this vintage machine, and more than likely add her to his collection. Hawk loved all things old, especially older cars.

Someone just about burned me up. I needed some lubricant under my boot, yet they ignored it for the pleasure of a woman. He knew that there was heat to the engine just before it had been injured. The person who had owned it before Hawk picked it up at an auction house had been horrific to the beautiful thing. The old car would be running again soon, he hoped. He wanted to see this thing out on the open road again.

"Where else do you hurt, baby?"

Hawk heard someone say his name, but he for the most part ignored it. He was busy and was pretty sure that whoever it was knew it. The sign on the door would have stopped most people when they read Stay The Fuck Out. But then, Samuel wasn't most people.

"Hawk, Vinnie needs you." Hawk turned to look at Samuel. There was fear there, and he took his hands off the car with an apology to it. Hawk was wiping down his hands as Samuel continued. "He was contacted by a friend of his, and she's in major trouble. He needs you to be his ground crew. They both—he and Abbie—are in the sky looking over the city now."

"Where?" Hawk was already moving toward his car when Samuel spoke again. He turned slowly. "Where did you say?"

"Erie County, New York. He said that you had a history there." That was an understatement if there ever was one. "That's why he sent me to find you and not just contact you. I'm supposed to give you this."

Hawk knew what it was as soon as Samuel put out his hand. He wasn't sure he wanted to touch it, but knew that in order to help his friend, he'd need it. Hawk looked at Samuel, not touching the beautifully-carved gold stone that lay in his hand. The chain alone was worth more than he had in his bank right now.

"She's not human." Samuel nodded. "I've never met her, but I know a great deal about what she is. Did he tell you anything about her?"

"All he told me was that you could find her when no one else could, and that it was important to everyone that you did." Hawk nodded. "What is she?"

"A sun goddess." Hawk said the name with reverence. A goddess of any kind was something that frightened him to no end, but this woman, this goddess, was scary all on her own. "She is said to be able to heat the world to nothing. To be able to kill a man with just a look. She is, in a word, scary. Anyone fucking with her has to have some major balls. Or a brain the size of a pea. More than likely both. A goddess of the sun is no one to fuck with."

"A goddess?" Hawk nodded and shut the door to his car as soon as he opened it. If Vinnie needed him to help find the goddess, his car would do him no good. "I must shift and take to the skies. Will you see to my baby here? Cover her up and store her for me?"

"Yes. You know that I will." Hawk nodded and looked at the medallion still in Samuel's hand. "Will you take it? I know that you'll have a connection to it, but there's no hope for it, Vinnie said. She means a great deal to him, apparently."

"I have no choice." As he reached for it, he had a thought that Samuel too would have her connection, and wondered what the big lion would be able to do now. The touch of the stone, her stone, had been the downfall of many. Samuel, he knew, would not be touched by the madness. Vinnie had told him a great deal about his friend...not her name of course—Hawk didn't do well with names—but everything else about her.

The touch was cold at first. Hawk took it into his hand and felt it warm up. As soon as the stone heated his hand to the point of pain, he had what he needed, but still he held it. Closing his eyes, he saw her even as he shifted to soar above the trees.

She is injured. By...magic that is not hers. Hawk moved closer to her in his mind and saw that she'd been not just hurt, but nearly killed. Her fire burned to repair her, but she was much too close to water to heal properly. It was cooling her faster than she could heal herself. *I can see her near a body of water, a large one by the looks of it. There is a forest that will soon burn if no one comes for her. Her breathing is slow, but I'm not sure if it's more to do with the fact that she's hurt or that she's slowing her body down to heal.*

Can you tell me if she's being followed or not? There might be a man. He'd have a scar on most of the left side of his face. There will be magic around him, not white but black. As black as you can think of. He told Vinnie she was near shutting down to conserve energy. *Abbie wants to know if you're coming.*

No, I can't go that far as my hawk. I've been working in the garage and that takes a lot out of us both. But there is someone. A man is coming for her. I can't see him, Vinnie. I can feel his hatred of her, but can't see him because of the aura that surrounds him. He focused on the man's face, trying hard to make it out, but all he could see was the scar. *He has been burned by her before, that much I can see. His face wears the marks of her touch.*

I'm telling Abbie now. When Vinnie came back to him, he'd been laughing, and that made Hawk smile. Vinnie was one of his best friends, and he loved the man's sense of humor. *She said that you should come to us now. That if she tears into this guy, she might need you to pick her teeth clean.*

Hawk nodded and moved in the direction of where the dragons were. He had lied to his friend about being able to fly that far, and he was pretty sure that Vinnie knew it. There were too many memories of his hometown that he just didn't want to bring up again. Erie County was a place that had never held any good things for him. As he spread his wings and moved east, he wondered if things were going to be any different, and knew that they wouldn't be. His parents still lived there. Maybe he'd be lucky and they'd be gone, and he could have a nice visit with the household cook and butler...the people who had made his survival easier as a kid.

Hawk had been an only child. Which, he supposed, was lucky for any other siblings that might have been born before or after him. His parents, Frederick and Bambi Hawkmen, had never wanted anyone to mar their perfect life. But a child, he'd heard someone say about his parents, had made them a much softer couple. Whatever the hell that meant, since all he'd ever felt from them was stone cold hatred. And he had been a blot on their life since the first time he had showed them what he could do.

A recessive gene, they'd been told when he'd been taken to the doctors to have his magic taken from him. And when the man said it was more than likely from the mother's side, he'd been fired, his license revoked, and his entire family put up for ridicule. No one put his parents in a slot with others. They were as perfect as the word implied. Nothing would ever dare mar their lives. His parents did not want to hear that they were at fault for his deformities.

As he grew older, from toddler to teenager, his abilities were harder and harder for them to hide, so they hid him instead. It had gotten so bad at one point that his mother, his dear sainted mother, had hired a man to kill him while he was playing on the ball field. And had Hawk not moved when he had, the bullet meant to take his head off would have ended her misery once and for all. But it did make cutting his ties with them so much easier a few days later. So at sixteen he'd left them arguing with the hit man about payment.

Hawk, are you still with us? Hawk had to shake his body to rid himself of the terror of his thoughts to answer Vinnie. *There are two bodies of water here, and neither of them seem to be hot. I know we're close, but I don't want to land to search for her if we don't have to.*

Her body lies with a crest of waterways. You should…do you see the two lakes? Where they are the closest they can be without touching? Vinnie told him he did. *At the tip of Lake Erie you will see a stand of trees. She is beneath them. The water is keeping her cooled. I think it is why she cannot heal herself.*

She can't heal herself, I'm thinking, but I can help her…there are the lakes. Okay, I see it now. Vinnie laughed. *You are good, my man. I see her body now. I will carry her to somewhere safe. I have spoken to Samuel. He has agreed for us to take her there, to the large barn at the back of his property. Are you using it?*

I am, but you must take her there. The man who follows her path is on his way. He's following her heat. Vinnie asked if he was taking care of him. *I will detain him, but not kill him. I know that she's your friend, but he's done nothing to me. I cannot harm him in any way.*

I understand. I just appreciate any help you can give us with this. This guy means harm to someone that is dear to me. We'll see you back at the house then. Hawk told him he would. *I know how hard it was for you to think of this place again. You're coming here, I can tell. Are you going to go and see them?*

No. I will not if I can avoid it. But he knew that he would. It was something that he did when he was feeling lost...go and see his parents, or at least where they lived. And to visit with his friends there. He never spoke to his parents, only watched them from afar. *I will see you soon.*

The car that was going for the girl was easy to deal with. When it stopped with his passengers at a light, Hawk asked the car, a big SUV, to help him along. The car asked in return that Hawk find him a part that he so needed, and Hawk assured him that he would. When the car sputtered and stopped running, Hawk thanked him again and left for the house he'd grown up in.

Landing in a big tree at the end of the property, Hawk watched the house. It had changed very little in the years, but it did look different. The pool was a new addition, he noticed. The trees surrounding the house were much bigger, and one of them—the one he'd used to climb out of his room when he needed freedom—was gone. Moving closer to the house, Hawk made his way to the one place where he knew he could enter the home, and slipped into the small broken brick as a mouse. As soon as he was inside, he shifted back to human and moved to the stairs. He was one of the few shifters he knew that could keep his clothing when he went from animal to human again.

Touching the rail, he knew that his mother had been down here recently. Hawk did wonder why...there was nothing of fashion down here. She'd never do her own wash, and storing things was not her job. Hawk moved up the stairs to the door to the kitchen. As he moved up the stairs, he knew why she'd ventured down here. She'd been hiding a gift for his father...a watch that he'd wanted for a long time. Like he needed another one.

With a touch to the lock, he opened the door and moved inside. There was no one in the big kitchen. The memories of this room, all of them good, made him smile. On the large table in the middle were several loaves of homemade bread, still steaming from the oven. *It must be Wednesday*, he thought with a smile. Her baking day. As he stood wondering if he should slice him a piece, Margo, the old cook, walked into the room. She didn't even pause in her movements to the counter with her beans from her garden. But as soon as she put them in the sink, she turned to him.

"Master Hawk." He was pulled to her ample bosom in a bear like hug, which was always surprising to him, knowing what she was as a shifter. Hawk had always loved this old woman, and hugged her as tightly as she did him. When she pulled back from him, he could see the tears.

"I have missed you too." She waved him off as she moved to the counter. When she turned, the large knife in her hand made him sit down at the table. It was her bread slicing knife, and he knew he was going to get an unexpected treat. "If you tell me this is for some party and I can't have any, I'm going to cry like I used to when you teased me with such a lie."

"No parties here for a few more days, and we'll not be working it, I think. But you and I, we'll have some ripe jam too. And before you wonder, they're gone. The two of them ran off just this morning." He nodded and watched as she sliced thick slices of the hot bread for them both and then handed him the tub of butter. "Make sure you put enough on them to soak them. You know how I love it."

He put enough butter on her slice to have her arteries clogging. When the door opened, the one that came from the garage, Hawk knew that Deacon, Margo's husband, had come to join them. His slice of bread wasn't buttered, but smeared with apple butter he had set on the table before washing his hands. He gave Hawk a hardy handshake and a good pat on the back. Hawk had missed this from the two of them.

"You well, boy?" Hawk nodded, and he took a healthy bite of the bread. "Heard tell you'd been killed some time back. It was in all the papers. We figured that your parents done had that done. No cause for that as far as we could see. You never bothered them no more."

"I read it too." He ate his slice even as Margo sliced several more for them. "Do you know if I had a nice funeral? Did any of my friends show up?"

He didn't have any friends and they all knew it. At least none that lived around here. Deacon smiled and nodded. He told him of the huge crowd that had come by after the graveside services, and that he and his missus had had to clean up after them when they'd come back here to have their social hour.

"You really are doing well? No mate yet?" Hawk shook his head. Deacon and Margo had known what he was from birth. Both of them were shifters too, but not like him. He was what had been referred to as an elite shifter. Hawk could shift into anything.

"No one. Vinnie and I are still together. He has himself a mate now. You'd like her. She's a golden dragon." Both of them were impressed and sent their love to the big dragon and his family. "I have a pride now. Not really mine, but a man that I admire and respect. His name is Samuel. Samuel Payne. His pack has a rag-tag group of different species, but he is fair."

"Good man, you say? Treats the people who are under him with understanding then?" Hawk nodded as he devoured his fourth piece of bread. "We're looking. Me and the missus, we're looking for a place to call home. These people your parents are turning away, tossing out of their 'pack,' they'll come your way in the next few months, we figure. Your parents don't think we know it yet, but we heard they were looking for replacements."

Hawk felt his anger surge forward. It was one thing to turn him out, but these people had made his stay here, his life here as a younger man, bearable. He wondered if his parents had any idea what this couple did for them daily. He doubted that they even knew their names, and they'd worked for his parents for at least the thirty years of his life.

"I'll talk to Samuel. I'm sure he won't have a problem with it. His mate, Kennedy, is Irish, and her grandmother, Lady Dani, is a hoot. You'll love them." Deacon thanked him and asked him how long before he knew. "You think they plan to move you out that quickly?"

"I do." Deacon looked at his mate before continuing. "Last week we were told that we'd no longer be living in the little house. Me and the missus had ten days to find us somewhere else to live. We had to move into a hotel."

"You'll come stay with me. I have a place. It's really too big for me alone, and I'd love to have you there." Deacon stood up, and Hawk could feel his sorrow. "You'll go now and be there in a couple of days, all right?"

"We'll leave today. There's nothing here to keep us. We'd only been...we was kinda hoping you'd come to see us once more before we got gone." Hawk nodded and wrote down his address. Deacon said they'd leave within the hour, when the house was locked up. He figured that they'd be there in a couple of days at the very least.

As Hawk took to the skies again, this time with a much lighter heart, he made his way to his house rather than back to the garage where Samuel let him store the cars and such. As soon as he landed in the yard, he looked around. This would be good for Deacon and Margo. He thought they'd like it much better than his parents' house. They might even be able to get that tangle of a garden under control.

"Anyone would like it much better." He moved to the door and pressed his hand against the wood. No one could enter his home without his permission. And that was what had kept him safe wherever he went. Hawk was nothing if not cautious.

CHAPTER 2

Vinnie sat very still as he watched Awnia rest. She wasn't human yet, and might not be until she was fully healed, but he watched her. When someone came into the garage—really a large barn—he turned to protect her, but relaxed when he saw Samuel coming toward him.

"How is she?"

Samuel never got close enough to see the goddess, but stayed back by the door. Vinnie had told him he could come closer, but he had said he felt better back where he was. This time he came about half the distance between the door and Awnia. Every time he came in, he got just a little closer to her. For some reason that made Vinnie laugh.

"She's much better. Still resting. Did you explain to Kennedy why she can't come to the house?" Samuel nodded but frowned. "She still wants me to move her, I take it."

"You know she does. She can't stand the fact that she's out here and not in a bed. I told her to come out and see for herself, but she said she'd wait until Awnia can meet her properly. The woman is going to drive us all crazy until this one is healed." Vinnie understood that. He wanted her healed as well.

Kennedy could get her Irish up better than anyone he knew. And when she had her mind set on something, there was no dealing with her. He loved the big lion to death, but mostly he wanted to smack her. Grinning, he told Samuel to come to him. If he could see her, maybe he could explain it to Kennedy.

"I can't do that. I know it's dumb to be afraid of her like this, but when I heard sun goddess, all I could think of was her being hotter than hell and burning me to death." Vinnie laughed. "Yeah, I told you, dumb."

"For the record, she can do all that and more. Not to scare you or anything, but she is very powerful. But I want you to take her picture and take it to Kennedy. That way she'll see why she can't come to the house until she's healed." Samuel looked torn but still stood where he was. "What if I told you that if she finds out that you're helping her, she'll make sure you're rewarded?"

"You know I don't care about that." Vinnie knew that about his friend too. "Just want her well, that's all. And by the way, there are a pair of shifters in the pride now. Their names are Margo and Deacon Hobbs. They're living with Hawk."

"I know them." Samuel nodded and Vinnie noticed that he'd halved the distance from where he'd been. "They used to cook at Hawk's family home. About the only two people I respect more than you. They saved his life a few times."

"Yeah, Hawk told Kennedy once that he wasn't on the best of terms with his parents. I'm assuming that they're not alive?" Vinnie knew that they were but said nothing to Samuel's fishing. "I guess he's none too happy that they've been cooking and cleaning for him since they arrived. He said it's like living in a dust storm, she's kicked up so much of it. He said his intentions were for them to live with him, not work for him."

"That sounds like them. In a week or so his yard will look like a showcase and his house will be spotless, with all the beds with sheets on them." Vinnie laughed at the memory of going to Hawk's house and staying over. It had taken them an hour to find sheets for the beds. "Margo cooks like it's her job, and puts up her own jams and jellies too."

Samuel stood staring at Awnia. Vinnie watched Samuel for any sign that he was afraid still, but he only stared at her. When he took a step back, Vinnie asked him if he wanted to take her picture.

"No. That doesn't seem right. I'll let Kennedy know that she's better off out here." He looked back at Awnia. "Is that her true form?"

"Yes."

Vinnie looked down at the woman he'd known for thousands of years. Her body was human-like in that she had a body, arms, and legs, but she was injured now and she was molten hot, and seemed to shift under the heatwaves that surrounded her. Her face was what stopped men in their tracks when they came upon her. It was beyond anything considered beautiful. Words failed to describe her. All he could say was that her eyes were as blue as the oceans and her hair was as red as the lava that ran in her veins as blood.

"What hurt her?" Vinnie moved to her head and rolled her to her side. Him being a dragon, he could touch her when she was like this, but not for long. Her heat was hotter than the breath his dragon spewed. "Christ, that looks nasty and painful. Who the hell did that to her?"

"I think she calls him Hatter. I'm not sure of all the details about him, but she says that he's mad with his supposed power. He is strong, I guess, if he could do this, but he's going to pay. I think he more than likely had help and had someone else hit her with magic. She'll heal from this, but it might take her a few days to a week. Oh, and I've made sure that no one will be able to find her heat from the air. The top of this barn is covered in a thick metal that can withstand the heat from her. They would usually find her if they were to look for her heat signature. It's why we had to work so quickly to get her to safety." Samuel asked him what magic they'd used to hurt her. "Something that would be ice-like. A shard of it would be able to pierce her and do damage to her badly. It would have killed her had it chilled her. Her body would have turned to stone, and there would be no healing from that."

Vinnie looked at the two large burns in her back. The one at her shoulder wasn't as bad as it could have been had their aim been just a little better. But the one at her midsection was worrying him. It had been deep, piercing her lung on the right side as well as her kidney. He'd been blowing heat on it ever since he'd brought her here, but it didn't seem to be doing much good. At least not that he could see.

After Samuel left, Vinnie sat on the floor and talked to Awnia. He'd been doing it since he'd found her and found that it calmed him a great deal. Smiling, he thought of the first time he'd seen her.

"You were fighting off those soldiers. Two of them had it in their head that raping you would be a sport." He laughed again. "I wonder what you might have done to them had they gotten that far. You were a little on the pissed side by then."

It had been quite a few hundred years ago, give or take a thousand or so. He'd been alone for a while by then and had nearly gone by the fight because he didn't want to get involved. But as he glanced away from the fight and the girl, he'd seen what she was…a spark in the otherwise horrible things around them. Vinnie thought that he'd try to reason with them before she hurt them.

"Please, you don't know what she is going to do to you." The biggest soldier looked at him and laughed. "She can kill you if you don't back off."

Why he'd tried to help them had never been clear to him. What he did know was that if she decided it was finished, nothing, including him, would survive it. The big man cupped his cock and balls and spoke to him.

"I know just what she's going to do for me. I'm going to have me a dip in that pussy of hers and she's going to scream like she likes it." He lashed the whip out again, this time catching Awnia on the cheek. But instead of blood pouring from the wound, they saw red hot lava. "What's this?"

It was too late. Vinnie didn't leave her but did shift. His dragon took him quickly, even as he moved toward the woman. When he snatched her up in his claws, the burn of her nearly had him drop her. But he held her until they were a safe distance from the now dead men. Vinnie shifted back to his human self and stared at the beautiful woman as she begged him to cook her with his breath. Vinnie shifted again and did as she'd asked. It had taken him a long time to get over blowing fire over a human being.

"You saved those people. Not the men, but the villagers. You saved them when I would have killed them. I thank you for that. I was angered and didn't watch what I was doing. Those other men had to go, however." She bowed before him. "I am in your debt."

"My debt?" She stood and looked at him when he laughed. "You are a goddess. I am the one who is indebted to you. I have never seen such a person as you. Never thought to touch one either."

She looked down at his legs, and there was no hiding that she'd hurt him. When she took a step toward him, Vinnie took one back. The thought of her touching him sort of frightened him a little, even after what he'd done to bring her here.

"Just a touch." He stood still while she moved again. "I shall not hurt you, young dragon. I mean only to heal what I have done to you."

Her touch, while very warm, didn't burn him as he'd expected it to. Instead, it heated his legs and feet much like he was in a hot bath or a pool of water heated by his breath. As soon as she stepped back, he could see what it had cost her to heal him, but that too, the burns to her own legs and feet, disappeared within moments.

"I'm called Awnia. I've no surname, as I've rarely had the need, but Solis is one that I use when necessary." He nodded and told her his name. "Well, Vicente MacIntyre, you have done me a great service this day. I have returned the service with a little of myself."

He hadn't known what she'd meant then, and still sometimes forgot what she'd given him. The gift of healing had been passed from him to his mate and any future children they would have. His kind, as most shifters with magic, couldn't heal themselves without causing great harm to themselves. But he could now, thanks wholly to her.

After that, and for a great many decades, the two of them had moved around the world together, until about a hundred years ago. Then she'd just disappeared from his life and he'd not heard from her again.

"What happened? Why did you leave me?" He didn't expect an answer, and even if she was awake she might not have answered him anyway. There was very little he knew about the goddess. And what he did know was snippets of things she'd said in conversation.

At dusk he left her. He had to go to his mate, and there were things he had to do as well to keep Awnia safe. He sent both Doul and Yve, his faeries, to watch over her. He knew that neither of them would cause her harm nor allow anyone who was a threat near her.

~~~

Hawk was under the hood of his car when he heard Vinnie. He was up to something, and before he could get out from his newest baby, the man came stomping into the garage where Hawk was.

"Hawk." The shout was enough to send the birds in the rafters to flight. "Hawk? Where the hell are you? I need you now. Samuel said you were…Hawk, answer me."

Hawk slid the dollies out from under the car and stared at his friend. He might have laughed at him, but decided he might be able to fix this car sooner if he stayed in one piece. When he looked at him, Hawk had to work hard not to even grin.

"You've been busy." Vinnie growled but said nothing. "I'd say that you were caught somewhere you shouldn't have been. And maybe…did someone shoot you?"

"Yes. That damned farmer down the road from you. He said that we were…that we were…. What was he doing out with a gun at his age?" Hawk wondered for all of a second what he might have been doing, then noticed that Vinnie's shirt was done up all wrong and that his pants were inside out. He must have realized it as well. "We're breeding, and she needed to…why are you laughing at me? You should be out there right now making his gun not work."

"Do you have any idea how complicated a gun is?" When Vinnie growled again, Hawk stopped bothering trying to hide his humor. "Christ, do you and Abbie ever not have sex? I've never seen two people forever trying to find a quiet place to fuck."

"I told you, we're breeding. It does something to the female when she is like this. Sex keeps her calm and happy…and me too, if you want to know the truth. And that man…I want you to go down there and break that gun. He could have hurt Abbie." Vinnie straightened his clothing as Hawk stood up. He was nearly finished anyway. "I also had a plan to come and see you anyway. What do you know of a man by the name of Pruitt? I think his first name might be Vega."

His skin turned icy cold and his heart began to pound so hard that he put his hand over it to calm it. Vinnie was saying his name, he could hear him, but the ability to respond was lost to him for the moment. Then everything went black.

When he found himself with his head between his knees and his world upside down, he knew that Vinnie would demand an explanation for Hawk passing out on him. But how did one tell a story so horrific it still, after all these years, gave him nightmares?

"I'm all right now." He wasn't, but Vinnie let him up. Samuel was standing there as his big lion, and Hawk wondered how long he'd been inside of his own head. "I guess you figured out that I know him."

"Yeah, got that. Mother fuck, you scared the shit out of me. I've never actually seen someone faint before. You certainly did it with style." Hawk nodded. He started to stand up, to go to his cars for comfort, but his legs were still wobbly and he stayed where he was.

"He's a man from my past. A man...to call him a man is to say that Samuel is merely a kitten. This man is a monster. One who preys on anything and anyone who can make him something. And when he is finished, you are dead." He looked at Vinnie. "How do you know him?"

"He called here. I don't know what he thinks he knows, but he wanted to know if I had any new recruits I wanted to pass his way." Hawk didn't understand, but Vinnie continued before he could ask. "He said he was in the procurement business. He took unwanted animals and put them to work. It took me a minute or two to understand he meant paranormals. Then I just hung up on him. How the hell did he figure out that some lived here?"

"More than likely he's had his eye on you for a while. I would say that he's known about you from a distance, and is now looking for your goddess. There's a good possibility that he might know that she's here." Vinnie shook his head. "Then someone else is new to your group? Or...."

Hawk stood up and started to pace. No way had the man known about Margo and Deacon. But his parents would know where they went. And even if they didn't know about them, they certainly knew about him.

"What is it?" Samuel was still pulling on his shirt as he spoke, having shifted back to his big normal self. "Is there some sort of danger we should know about this man? We need to protect our families if there is."

"He's danger. I would say more than you might be able to handle without a lot of help." He looked at Vinnie. "Your goddess might be in danger. I was wrong. He probably doesn't know about her, but he will if he comes here looking for Margo and Deacon. I'm sorry. I never thought about it when I invited them to live here. My parents would know where I live, and that Margo and Deacon would come to me when they left. I have no idea why they'd care, as they were about to fire them anyway."

"There is no reason to be sorry. We know now and we'll work with what we have." Samuel looked at him hard. "You'll have to share how you know him. I'm sorry. I know that it's painful for you, but it might help us to know what sort of man we're up against."

"The worst sort of man. And he's a practitioner of black magic. He takes others, men and women like us, and sells us to the highest bidder. But not before he…he has his piece of the pie." Hawk took a long slow breath before he pulled his shirt off and turned. "My parents took me to him so that he could take my abilities out of me. I was there a month before I was able to escape. And if not for Margo and Deacon, I would never have made it. He did things to me, things that I'll never share with you beyond what I show you now. But you should know that if I find him near anyone I know, I'm going to kill him. Plain and simple."

"Christ." Hawk pulled his shirt down when Samuel spoke. When he turned, he couldn't even look at the man for fear of what he'd see there. But when he said his name, Hawk had no choice but to look. "You're not going to be hurt by him again. I swear to you. We're family here and we take care of our own."

"I can take them someplace else. He might not come here if they're all he's looking for. But—"

Vinnie cut him off. "You'll do no such thing. They will stay put. And if Margo is still making bread like she always did, she might come stay with us for a while. Man, that woman can cook." Hawk smiled and Vinnie laughed. "You think I'm kidding? I love that woman."

"She's the closest thing to a mom I've ever had, and if you come near her, I'll sic Deacon on you. He loves his wife with his life." Hawk knew that both men would understand that. They loved their own mates the same way. "I have to let them know he's here. They'll need to take precautions. I'm hoping that my parents still have no idea that they're shifters too. It might keep them safe for a bit longer. Pruitt will know, of course. Why else would he come here? Other than to get me too."

"We all need to know that he might be coming here and keep safe. But we have to talk before we take this to the pride." Hawk nodded. "And if you think that Deacon and Margo could add something to the conversation, please invite them as well."

"I think...this is Wednesday. Baking day. Why don't I see if you all can come to my house? It might be easier on them. Margo tends to flutter when she's nervous, and having to entertain will help her out."

"Flutter?" Hawk nodded at Samuel, and Vinnie laughed. He knew that Samuel had spoken to both Deacon and Margo, but just over the phone. He was in for a surprise when he actually met them. "Okay then. Let me know. I'll see about gathering the rest of them up and we'll wait to hear from you."

Hawk waited until both men were gone before he started to clean up around the cars. He thought about simply reaching out to the older couple, but knew that it was a coward's way out. Hawk knew that he should speak to them in person. As soon as he was finished, he shifted and ran to the house rather than fly. The wolf in him seemed to enjoy the run as much as he did. As soon as he got to the house, he knew that something had happened.

"Your mother called here." Hawk sat down when Margo continued to knead the dough she was working. He almost felt sorry for it. The dough looked like it was being worked by a wrestler. "She said she'd contacted that monster for you. I don't think she's happy that we left without notice."

"I should have thought that she'd retaliate." Margo shook her head and told him it was fine. "Samuel and the pride would like to talk to us about him. He needs as much information as we can give him."

"You tell them to come here. I've been baking like it's my job." He nodded and told her he thought she'd say that. "I've some stew on too. Some of the beef that was in the ice box in that pantry. There's a pie or two as well that I can whip up."

"I'll tell him." He reached for Samuel and simply told him to be there at six. It was just after three now. "He said that there would be ten more for dinner. He wants to know if he can bring anything."

"Good heavens no. I have to fill my time now, don't I?" She gave the bread a good pat and told him to shoo. He'd never really understood that word, but knew what she wanted him to do. As he left the kitchen, all sparkling clean since she'd gotten there, she called him back. "Hawk, he'll never hurt you again. I will lay down my life for you if it comes to that. Neither of them will hurt you. I promise you that I'll die first."

"You won't have to. Samuel said that he might need our help, but he will protect us all." Margo nodded and waved him out of the room. Hawk moved to his office to work. The thought of going to work on his cars was not what he needed. He wanted to occupy his mind by other means.

Hawk thought about calling his parents, to ask them why they would do such a thing to such wonderful people as the Hobbs. But he also knew that his parents had never thought of their servants as people, but things. Ones that cleaned up when they were supposed to and were out of sight when not. Hawk wondered, even after all this time, if his parents even knew their names. After he'd sat there for nearly an hour, he reached for the phone. It was time to call in a few favors.

He called his lawyer first. There were things this man knew that could and would make it hell for his parents. When he'd left, Hawk had made it his business to find out all he could about them. The man seemed excited to finally get to work.

"I need you to send them the video, the one where they're telling the world that I'm dead." Gay Mendoza had worked for his parents for a long time, and now worked for him. "They're threatening my friends and that just won't do. I would like for them to realize that this shit is going to stop."

His laughter made Hawk smile. "I can do that. I doubt that they'll take it seriously, but I will send it to them. What else? Because I'm thinking that after all this time, you have a lot of ideas on how to put them in their place. By the way, I have the will that your grandmother made. Did you know that you're the sole heir to her estate? Your parents were to get nothing. They've been living on your dime, buddy."

"Really? That's interesting. So on top of everything else, insurance fraud. Can we make this work in my favor? Also, there are the pictures that I gave you. I'd like for you to send them those as well." There was silence at the other end, and he thought maybe Gay was going to refuse.

"You do know that it's going to be a shit storm when they get those, right?" Hawk told him he knew. "Good. I'm glad you're finally doing this. And about your death? What would you like to do about that?"

"Why, I think it's time that I was brought back to life, don't you? And I'd very much like for you to evict the freeloaders. I've had enough of their shit. I have a friend that'll help you. I'll have her call you."

Gay was still laughing when they hung up. This was going to make a lot of waves, and not a few of them could come back and bite him in the ass. But they were fucking with his friends, as he'd told Gay. Next, he called the only other elite shifter he knew. William Bonneville, Big Will to his friends.

"My parents are at it again." The man didn't say anything, but then, Big Will rarely did. "I was wondering if you'd like to come and visit. Margo would love to make you some of her famous rolls and tea."

"You still in the same place?" He told him he was. "Be there tomorrow. I'll stay with you, right?"

"Yes. I'll have you a room set up the way you like it." The line went dead.

Hawk moved from his office to the kitchen again, to see Deacon peeling potatoes. The man was singing to the radio at the top of his lungs, and Margo was pulling bread from the oven…if he counted correctly, fifteen loaves.

"Big Will is coming here tomorrow." Hawk had waited for a pause in the music to make his announcement. "Would you mind helping me with his room?"

"I've taken care of it. We thought you'd be calling him here." Deacon winked at his wife. "And we've a batch of those rolls he likes in the fridge right now."

Nodding, he left them. He should have known they'd be on top of things. Smiling, he left for the garage. He felt like he could work now. His parents were going to have a cow within the next few days. And Hawk was looking forward to it.

CHAPTER 3

Awnia rolled to her back gently. It hurt, but not like it did when the blast had hit her. Looking around the cavernous room, she wondered where Vinnie might have taken her. Sitting up as slowly as she could, she pulled the blanket up to her bare breasts and looked around with her magic just to make sure that she wasn't in harm's way.

"You need to rest." Awnia looked over at the young woman who only just came out of the shadows. "Vinnie won't be happy if you have a relapse. He worked really hard to keep you safe."

"I won't. I'm better now." She started to stand but remembered that she was naked. "I don't suppose you have some clothes I can borrow?"

The woman nodded to a bag that was just behind her. Awnia pulled it to her as the woman sat down. She knew that she was a vampire and that she had recently fed, but nothing more about her.

"I'm Clar. My husband is Stephen. I think you might know him." Awnia told her she knew of him but had not met him. Letting the blanket fall, she pulled the shirt over her head and then stood up to pull on the soft pants. "I didn't know what you'd wear so I brought you a little of everything. There's a skirt in there if you'd rather have that."

"This is fine. Thank you very much." She pulled the pants on, keeping a firm grip on the wall beside her. "I am Awnia. Awnia Solis. Do you know where Vinnie is? I've tried reaching him, but he must be his animal. I cannot reach him when he is not human."

"He's with his mate. They're...she's breeding." Awnia nodded. She knew that dragons needed sex desperately when they were having a young one. "I'm to take you to the big house if you want. I'm sure that they'd really like to meet you. And we're going to Hawk's house for dinner. Do you know him?"

Awnia shook her head. She wondered briefly if there would be someone she could get some much needed help from. But if Vinnie was nearby, he'd help her out. Maybe. He had a mate, so it might not work. Awnia looked at the woman again when she was dressed. There was something about her that was familiar...not herself, but what she was. But she couldn't put her finger on it. There was the vampire, of course, but there was something more.

"I should like to touch you, if you don't mind." The woman didn't move, but she didn't run either. "You know what I am, am I correct? If you do then you know that, with your permission, I won't harm you."

"Vinnie told us." She put her hand out, but it was shaking a little. "I know that you would never hurt me. Not unless...I won't do anything to piss you off."

"I'm very sure that you won't." Awnia touched her hand and felt the connection immediately. "You are a necromancer. A very good one too. I'm glad to know that. People need so much help, no matter what shape they're in."

"I've been helping Hawk. He has...his abilities are a little more advanced than mine, but we work well together." Awnia nodded, wanting to meet this Hawk person more and more. "He's also a shifter. I think that Vinnie said he's an elite shifter. Do you know what that means?"

"I do. He can shift into any animal or thing he wishes. There are not many of his kind left. I know one such man. But he is a loner for the most part, and has not been around for some time." Clar nodded and moved to the door. "I need to speak to Vinnie. I hurt very badly, and he's the only one who can help me with that."

"He said that he has to heat you with his dragon's breath. Is that right?" Awnia nodded and told her it was the only way she could cool off sometimes. "I would think that would be worse than the hurt you have right now, but then I'm not a sun goddess. I suppose you can stand a great deal of heat."

"Yes. But I can create more, too, if I need it." She didn't want the girl to think badly of her so she changed the subject. "I should like to meet the man who has housed me. He must be a very understanding person."

"Samuel Payne. And he is. His mate is Kennedy." They moved out of the barn and into the light. The sun felt wonderful on her face and arms, and she lifted her face to it fully. Clar said nothing as she waited, and Awnia was grateful. She needed this more than she could say. When she looked at the woman again, she saw that there was a hint of fear in her face.

"It's the sun." Clar nodded. "I told you I would never harm you, and I won't. I need the heat of the sun to heal in small ways. It is what I am."

"I understand. But you should know that you're glowing. And I mean really glowing."

Awnia nodded. She could feel it...her body hummed with the feeling from the rays. As they made their way to the house, Awnia was able to control her heat, but didn't close it down completely. It was dangerous, she knew, but for now, until she left, she had to be as strong as she could be.

The house was warm. Not in the sense that it was heated, but she could feel the love and happiness from it as soon as they entered. This sort of heat would heal her as well, but she didn't take it. To do so would drain the house and the people living there. And Awnia had no wish to harm those within. As soon as the big lion, the man of the house, came from one of the rooms, he stopped and stared at her. Awnia bowed before him.

"Master Samuel. I am in your debt for housing me." He didn't move when she stood up again. Her mirth bubbled out when he continued to stare at her for several minutes. "You have seen a woman before, I'm sure."

"Yes. But not one that had goddess as a title. I do call my wife that on occasion, but it's more of a term for her than her actual title." She liked this man. "You're also glowing a nice shade of gold. Shimmering gold, as a matter of fact. I'm assuming that means you're better?"

"Getting there." He came toward her, and she could see he was at a loss as to how to talk to her. She put him at ease, or so she hoped, by putting out her hand with a warning. "If you take my touch, however brief, we will be connected. Much like the connection you have with the others of your pride, but mine will be magical. I tell you this so you'll know...something of a warning, but in a nice way."

Samuel nodded and put out his hand. He wasn't shaking, but he was nervous. She touched his hand and found out a great deal about the young lion. He was not just a good leader, but a great one. A man she could take into her confidence.

"I'm being chased. Have you been made aware of that?" He said that Vinnie had told them all. "This man, he will bring danger to your pride. As soon as I am able, I will leave here. He will search but not harm if I'm not here, I think. If he does...then I will return and help you."

"We're making plans to keep you safe." She nodded. It had been said to her before. But when Hatter came, he didn't spare humans or shifters trying to help her, but killed them all. "You don't believe me. I understand. There is more to this man than we think, I'm sure, but we're a pride that is not your normal bunch of cats. I have...there are more here than that."

"I know. Cats, leopards, vampires. Even a bear or two, if I'm not mistaken. But this man, he is stronger than that, than any of that. He will not be kind or gentle. He wants me to come to him so that he can be rewarded. I'm betting that all he will get is his own death, but he thinks she'll be honorable. He might have the powers to do so...take me, I mean, but not fight Temptress." She looked around the big room they were in. "All this space cannot hold what I am in my truest form, yet Temptress, the woman who sired me, will fill ten times ten of this room and still over flow it. I am not as strong, not nearly as strong as I should be."

"How do we make you stronger?" She flushed, and he grinned. "Okay. I'm assuming that it's a little more involved than I can give you."

"Yes. A mate. Which I cannot have." He asked her why. "Because I have been cursed. My mother, as I said, is a jealous and vicious woman who will not allow me to mate. My powers would be greater than hers, greater than them all."

"And by all, do you mean other gods and goddesses?" Awnia nodded. "And that is a shit ton of magic, I'm betting."

"Yes. A very large shit ton." A woman entered the room, and she felt the connection to her through Samuel. "Your mate?"

"Yes. Kennedy, this is Vinnie's friend, Awnia. Awnia, my mate and wife, Kennedy Payne. And the young man behind her is my son, Kendal. He's just turned one."

"A fine man you are too." She looked at Kennedy, then back at the boy. "He is strong. Stronger than the two of you. He will be a greater man than the greatness of his father."

"Aye, you've the right of that. Ye be the goddess." Awnia nodded, not taking her eyes from the boy. He moved from behind his mother to stand beside her, and Awnia went to her knees.

"You know what I am." He nodded and put out his hand. "You cannot touch me unless your mother and father say yes."

Kendal looked at his mom, who looked at Samuel. She knew that they were talking. It was a big step for her to connect with the child. But she knew that the connection would not be the only thing that was exchanged between them.

"Our touch will be magic, Master Samuel. He will have a part of me, as you and the missus do, but he will be stronger for it. And he in turn will heal me. Not completely, but as complete as I can be without a mate." When Samuel asked her what she needed to do, she looked at him. "A touch, nothing more."

"I've no problem with ye making him stronger. But if he comes to harm because of it, I'll tear you apart, goddess or not." Samuel came to stand beside Kennedy, and he too gave his consent. The little boy put out his hand and touched her cheek. Then in an act completely mesmerizing to her, he leaned in and kissed her other cheek.

The pain shocked her. It started at the place where he'd touched his lips to her, then took over her body. Her breath felt as if it had been knocked from her, then someone squeezed her for good measure. Awnia fell back on the floor. Her back bowed from it as she was lifted up by some unknown force. The scream that wanted to spill forward seemed to make the pain worse, and she had no choice but to let it go. Then the blackness took her again.

~~~

"What do you mean, you've no idea what happened? She was right in front of you." Samuel was trying his best not to snap back at Vinnie, but the man was pissing him off. "And why the hell didn't someone call me when she woke up?"

"I've told you six times, and if you make me say it again after this, I'm going to shift and tear your ass up. She wanted to touch Kendal. I said yes, Kennedy said yes. Then when he kissed her cheek, it was as if she were possessed by something. Her body nearly bent in half and she rose up off the floor to the ceiling. Had I not been there to catch her, she would have crashed to the floor again when she passed out. Are you any more satisfied this time than you were the other times?" Vinnie growled. "Take it down a notch or two, or I will. I didn't contact you because there was nothing to say. She was awake. Silly me. I thought she'd told you."

"We can't talk any more. Not when I'm a dragon." Vinnie started pacing again, but it was less violent, calmer even. "She's never done that before. Touched a child, so far as I know. They hold a special power that she can use, but it drains the child. Kendal must be extremely strong for her to have been able to touch him."

"She didn't." Vinnie turned to him. "Awnia didn't touch Kendal. He touched her. Then he kissed her cheek. Kennedy and I talked about it. She didn't touch him at all."

"Then...I don't understand. You said she asked, but didn't touch him?" Samuel told him that Kendal touched her before she did. "And Kendal is all right? He wasn't hurt at all?"

"No. He's in the kitchen having a snack. If anything, he might have gotten a bigger appetite from it. She said that he'd heal her, but...I don't know, maybe that's why he's so hungry."

Samuel had been terrified when she'd screamed. Then when she lifted up, Kennedy grabbed their son and ran with him. Samuel was ready to follow them when Awnia suddenly fell from the ceiling and into his arms. After that, he'd brought her up here to lay her down and reached for Vinnie.

"That medallion I gave you, do you still have it?" He told him that Hawk still had it. "I'll have to get it back from him. She gave it to me decades ago to protect for her. It's a part of her. I'm not entirely sure what part, but it's my only connection to her. I think it keeps her from dying somehow."

"It does." When Awnia sat up, she looked dazed. "I have frightened you. I'm very sorry for that. The child, he is well?"

"Yes. Eating." Vinnie sat on the bed again, but was careful not to touch her. Kennedy had told Samuel that she didn't smell the goddess on him at all. He had expected her cat to get pissy, but she said that there was nothing to get mad about. "Are you okay now?"

"I don't know. I feel much better." She stood up and stretched. "Yes, much better indeed. I have not felt this well since…well, I don't remember how long."

Samuel watched her stretch again and wondered if she realized that she was no longer glowing but now seemed to be hot. Heat devils, he'd heard them called, danced over her body.

"Kendal said to tell you that he loves you. I don't normally tell strangers that my son loves them, but he made me promise." Awnia smiled at him with her thanks. "You have a fan in him, I think. Did he do this for you?"

"Yes. His touch, one of complete trust and purity, did it. I had never let a child touch me before. I…it was my plan to touch him, to help him keep safe. When he gave me the gift, the kiss, it was as if he had given me a great deal of energy. He is a very wonderful little man." Samuel nodded. He knew that already, but it was good to hear it from someone else. "Your wife? Is she upset with me?"

"No, not at all. She was worried when you doubled over, but not mad. Had Kendal been hurt, that might have been a different story." He cleared his throat, uncomfortable with threatening her. "We were getting ready to leave for Hawk's house. Are you well enough to come with us?" Samuel hoped so, and when she didn't answer him right way, he looked at Vinnie.

"She's trying to decide on something." Vinnie laughed when he backed up. "Not to hurt you, jackass, but if she should go or not. She's terrified of liking all of us too much and then getting us hurt."

"We'll need your help to make sure we're ready when this man comes for you. Do you have a name we might be able to try and do a search on?" She nodded, then frowned. "I'm sorry, you're probably exhausted."

"No. I'm fine. I don't know his name, this guy that is coming for me. I know you need the information, but I've only called him the Mad Hatter. It suited him somehow. He wears a hat, all the time. Mostly it is ball caps, but before, long ago when I first knew him, they were top hats, bright colors with flowers or feathers on them."

"A dandy?" Awnia shrugged but smiled. "You know something that might make it easier for us to find him? I'm sure that you don't have an address or anything like that."

"No, I don't have an address for him, but I did manage to mark him. Not long ago I was able to burn a scar onto him. His face. I had hoped it would go much deeper, but he...I was injured and wasn't able to finish him." Samuel wondered what had happened, but he thought that Vinnie knew when the big man shivered. "He was ill for a long time, and I had thought he would stop coming for me. But I should have known. I'm something that he wants very badly."

"For what?" She looked at him, and he was sure that she wasn't going to answer him. "I'm sorry. But it might help us to know."

"I understand. I do. If Hatter can capture me and take me to my mother, then she will reward him." Samuel asked her how he would be rewarded before he thought maybe he didn't want to know. "He will be a god. Not a strong god. But I don't think that's the point. It will give him powers that he doesn't have now, and he will be a god. The title is most important to him."

"And you? What will she do to you once she has you back? I'm assuming that there isn't a lot of love between the two of you." She grinned, and he thought it was the scariest thing he'd ever seen.

"None at all. She'll try and end me. And if she succeeds, which is likely, then she will take what is mine from me. Not just my powers, though those are great, but she will take my looks as well. She will, in effect, become me. But a much nastier, meaner me. Not that it matters, really. When I'm dead, she'll destroy all that is here. All of the world." Awnia went to the window. "It's why she has cursed me. Without a mate, a person to complete me in more ways than you can imagine, I will be at her mercy. At both hers and Hatter's mercy. I've no way of coming to my mate because of her calculations. If I'm stronger than her, you see, she will end."

"Ending you by killing you, you mean." She nodded but didn't turn. The heat still radiated off her, and he had a thought that Kendal had caused it. "Did my son do something to you? With his kiss, he did something to you to make you heat like this, correct?"

"Yes. He trusted. Temptress said no one would ever trust me. He did. It was the first time...no one has ever trusted me fully before. Even you, when I asked to touch him, didn't trust me. But I understand that." Awnia turned to look at Vinnie. "Not even my dragon trusted me fully. I could have killed him at any time, and it was always in the back of his mind. But Kendal had no such thoughts but to offer me comfort. And a bit of his own magic."

"How many curses must you overcome to become strong?" She looked out the window again. And this time he needed the answer. "Awnia? How many?"

"Two more. Just the two. One may happen now. But the love of a man will never come to me. I'm a sun goddess, after all." She turned then to look at him. "A man must be of a certain breed, without fault, without anger in his heart, just love. He must give me his all. When he comes to me, he will take a part of me into him, have it as his heart for all time. A man with magic of his own."

"And the other? The one that can happen?" She turned away again. He looked at Vinnie, who was staring at her as well. He knew, he was sure of it. But from the look on his face, he didn't like it any better than she did.

"She must be able to kill without thought." Vinnie looked at him as he continued. "She couldn't do that. Never. Not even when she was being hurt could she kill Hatter."

"And you can now?" She nodded. "Why? What's changed that wasn't there before? My family? This pride?"

"Your help. And that of your child." She came away from the window then and smiled at him. "You will help me, will you not, Master Samuel? No matter what I say or even if I leave, you will protect me."

"Yes." She touched his cheek then, and he felt her heat. Not burning, but a warmth that spread throughout his body. "You trust me as well?"

"I do. And as much as it terrifies me, if I do not stay, you will die. All of you." He didn't want to hear that and nearly told her so. "But with your help I might be able to beat Hatter. If not...if I do not, he will die with me. That should end the threat for all of you and your pride."

"I don't want you to die either, Awnia." She moved away from him and out of the room. Samuel looked at Vinnie. "She will, won't she? She'll die to protect us."

"She will, I think." He stood up. "The piece that Hawk has, it's not just to keep her alive, but her mate as well. I know that part. If he can wear the pendent, put it on his neck and let his heart consume it, she'll know that he's her mate. And the only reason I know this came not from her, but from Yve. She knew more about the goddess than even Awnia does."

"It's not that simple, is it? The fact that he can wear it, there's more, isn't there?" Vinnie shrugged. "What do you know? Please tell me, Vinnie. I need to help this woman. I have no idea why, but helping her is very important to me all of a sudden."

"That when he takes it within his heart, there will be a reckoning like no other. The gods and goddesses will come to her and bow before her. They will pay her homage. Her father, a god of little worth until then, will acknowledge her, take her and her mate under his wing for all time." Samuel nodded. He didn't really get it, but that it was going to be a huge deal he understood. "She will no longer walk the earth as a mortal person, but as a goddess that she truly is."

"How do we find her a mate?" Vinnie laughed. "You tried, didn't you? To wear it. What happened to you?"

Vinnie pulled his shirt up and showed the scar that he'd seen before. Samuel had always thought it was because of a fight he'd had with another of his kind, but when he looked closer, he could see that it was round, like the medallion that he'd given Hawk.

"It didn't work, in case you didn't get that. I nearly died when I put it on, and before she could get it off, it had nearly burnt to my heart. I thought...when it started to burn into my body, I thought it would work. But she screamed at me to take it off and, by then, it was too late." He asked him what it was supposed to do if not burn. "Absorb into me."

CHAPTER 4

Hawk walked along the property line. He knew that he should be back at the house helping Margo with dinner, but she had told him to get out from under her feet. Smiling, he thought about the flustered look on her face when he'd asked her what he could do.

"Be gone." Hawk had looked at her oddly, and she told him again. "I've enough going on without you under my wings. You've been...go out to the yard and fly. But leave me to my work. I'm nervous enough as it is."

So he'd come out here. And now, an hour later, he had no idea what he should be doing out here either. There were guests coming, the first to his house, and here he was looking at the flowers.

"It's considered bad form to walk by a person without speaking." He was startled to say the least, but when he turned to look at the woman who had spoken, he nearly swallowed his tongue. "You could, I suppose, just move on by. I'd not mind really, but I was afraid you'd step on the little ones. They've no wings as yet."

He looked to where she was pointing and knelt down. The little fairy flies were just hatched, he could see that, and their downy wings were not yet strong enough to carry them away. As Hawk touched the flower that they clung to, one of them moved to his finger and bowed before him.

"They're only a few hours old." She said she'd seen them hatch. "Really? What a rare treat. I've only seen it once before, long ago. However did you manage it?"

"I was sunning myself. I need the rays more lately. I think that it is due to the fact that I was so unwell before." He looked at her as the little fairy moved over his fingers. He saw nothing to lead him to believe she was anything but in the prime of health. "You're not afraid of me?"

"No. Should I be?" She didn't answer but looked at the flowers again. "You're the sun goddess. I saw you when I helped search for you. You do look a good deal better than before."

"I was nearly dead." She'd said it so matter-of-factly that he laughed. "You find me dying funny, sir?"

"No. Just the way you said it." The fairy moved off, joined by her family, their wings finally strong enough to carry her and her family away. "The pride is coming over to my home tonight to plan a way to keep you safe. I'm assuming they think you need it. I'm sort of nervous to have guests at my house." He had no idea why he'd said that to her, and felt a little foolish.

"Hatter is coming." He nodded, not sure who that was unless it was the man in the car. He'd never actually seen the man, but he had known where he was going. "When he comes here, he'll try and kill the pride. Their only recourse is to let me go, but I doubt that they will. Samuel is very stubborn."

"He is." Hawk stood up when she did. "I'm Russel Hawkmen. Everyone calls me Hawk. It's my favorite animal."

"A bird of prey." He nodded, not sure why he'd told her his full name. He'd never really been inclined to do that before. "But you're so much more, aren't you?"

"I can do a few things." Hawk took a step toward her. He'd never met a female that he could talk to so easily. And especially one that made him feel as if he was not some sort of freak. He found he wanted to smell her, bring her scent into his body, and then taste her. "Will you be coming to the house later?"

"Yes."

Her step back made her stumble, and he reached for her. In the back of his mind, he knew that touching her was wrong, but she'd been about to fall and he had to save her. But as soon as he put his hand on her arm, he felt everything about her. Hawk wanted her as well.

Hawk stared down at her for several moments while he continued to hold her. Her eyes darkened, and he wanted to pull her to him again. When he wrapped his other hand around her arm, she came to him willingly, but she was still stiff. Hawk didn't care so long as he could taste her.

"I'd like to kiss you." She shook her head but licked her lips. The moistness of them seemed to beg him to take them into his mouth, and he caught the lower one in his teeth. Letting it go, Hawk pulled her body flush with his. "Please. I only want a kiss."

"You should be hurting now." He wasn't and right now, wouldn't have cared if she shot him...touching her was all he could think about. "Are you going to kiss me or not?"

"Yes." Hawk lowered his mouth. Slowly and as gently as he could, he brushed his mouth over hers. Her lips were soft and still wet from her tongue, and he nibbled on them again. Then when he couldn't stand it any longer, he kissed her.

It was only meant to be one to taste her...a simple touching of his lips to hers. Something that would have him breathless, no doubt, but also leaving him with her taste and scent all to himself. But the moment that he deepened the kiss, ran his tongue along the seam of her lips, the second that she let him in, Hawk knew that nothing with this woman would be simple. Cupping her ass now, holding her body close to his, he moved to the closest object he could find and pressed her against it. The tree seemed to moan with their combined weight, and he lifted his head to look around.

"I need you." She nodded and pulled at his shirt. "I don't know what to do. Are you going to be all right if I drink from you?"

"I'm...I'm needy, but for only you. Do you know what that means?" Hawk shook his head. "Sex. I want to have sex with you more than anything right now. I feel...what are you?"

"Shifter." Hawk pulled her shirt up and filled his hand with her bare breast. "I need to be inside of you. I want to bury my cock deep inside of you and feel you come with me. I want to drink from you, taste your cream while you...Christ."

Dropping to his knees, he pulled her pants off. She was bare beneath them as well, and he buried his mouth over her pussy while he pulled her soft pants from her body. Her cream slid down his throat, filled his body. Sliding his fingers into her sheath, he relished the way she rode his hand and soaked him as he made a feast of her clit and nether lips. There was so much more of her juices than he could capture, so he lifted her leg to his shoulder and ate her hungrily.

Her climax filled his mouth again. As her cum dripped from his chin and onto his bared chest, he looked up at her. She was beautiful, and she was his.

Standing up, he pulled her hips up. His need to mark and to take her was making his breath hot in his lungs. Taking her to the ground, he leaned over her until he thought he could take her without hurting her. She looked up at him, and he could see the need reflecting back at him.

"I'm a shifter. When I take you...when I fill you with my cum, you're going to be marked by me. I'll bite you." She nodded and bared her throat for him. "You're my mate."

She stilled. Her breathing even seemed to stop, and she put her hands on his chest. Hawk watched her. He could see that she was thinking, trying to figure something out, but he had no idea what it might be.

"I'm no man's mate." He slid his cock into her heat and rolled his hips until she moaned. "Yes, please more. I want more. But I am not saying that we're...oh yes. Please, more, Hawk. It's just that I cannot take a mate. It is...I cannot have one."

"Fuck that." He slammed forward. Her release nearly took his breath away, and when he pulled to the tip to take her again, her legs wrapped around his hips so that when he pounded into her again, he was deeper, her sheath tighter around him. Leaning into her throat, he licked her pulse, felt the pounding of it under his tongue. When she cried out again, saying his name, Hawk lifted her ass up to meet his downward stroke and sank his teeth into her throat.

Blood filled his mouth, hot, boiling hot as it filled his veins and cells. He knew the moment that it touched his heart, the second that her blood filled it and then spread to the rest of his organs. His mind exploded with information about her, the man that chased her, her mother that wanted her dead. Taking more of her, drinking deeply of her, Hawk moaned when she dug her nails into his flesh, when she turned his head to hers and licked the same path he'd taken.

Her bite, deep and painful, brought him over the edge. His climax emptied not just his balls into her, but everything about him; whatever he was, whatever he'd ever be, she took it. A second, then a third climax had him taking her again, harder, faster, until he could no longer move from coming so many times. Hawk felt his vision blur, his body weaken, until he fell atop her and knew no more.

~~~

Awnia held Hawk to her. Never in all her life had she come so hard, felt so much, or wanted so much more than she did from him. As he lay on her, she ran her fingers over his body and felt what had been done to him. His wings, the wings of his hawk, would no longer be the same. When he lifted his head after a few more moments, she could see the dazed look on his face. She was sure she wore the same look as him.

"You're my mate." She shook her head. He had to have seen what that meant. How her mother would destroy him if it was even partly true. "You gave yourself to me. Drank from me as I did you. That has made us mates, bonded mates for all time."

"I cannot have a mate." He held her when she struggled to get from under him. He wasn't hurting her, but she needed to move. Rolling him to his back was what she thought she wanted until he put his hands on her hips and held her. Awnia sat up and moaned. "You're very deep."

"Yes." He rolled her hips, pulled her forward, then back, and she moaned. "Ride me, Awnia. I want to watch your face when you come again."

It was on the tip of her tongue to tell him she couldn't do that again, but he felt so good. His cock was so hard that she felt as if she could ride him forever. Rolling her hips forward again, she touched her finger to his nipple and watched it harden. As she leaned down the sensation of his cock touching her in a different way made her bite him harder than she'd meant. He didn't pull her back, but held her to him as she bit him again, this time drawing blood.

"Drink." She sucked harder from the tiny wound, then bit him again to drink deeply. Hawk rolled her to her back and held her head to him as he fucked her, his cock doing amazing things to her as his fingers toyed with her tight hole. The moment he breached the rosette, she threw back her head and cried out. The climax had been quick and hard.

"Again. Come for me again." Her body bowed up again; his blood dripped on her now from his wound, and she pulled him down to seal it. But when his mouth was near her breast, all she could think about was him biting her there. As soon as his fangs dipped into her flesh, she came again, then again when he pounded her into another climax. His own rush of cum as it filled her brought her for a third time.

They lay there this time with him beneath her. He must have rolled them over again when she closed her eyes, and now she looked down at him. His own eyes were closed, and she had a chance to look at him without him seeing her. But for some reason she knew that he was aware.

He had a classic face. It was one of beauty, if a man could be called that. His hair was short, almost too short for her taste normally, but for some reason she liked it on him. The scruff of his beard was soft to her finger, but she could feel the burn of it on her throat. His eyes were blue, she knew, intensely so, and she loved his mouth. And what it did to her when he touched it to her....

"My parents are still alive, and from what I got from your memories, they're not much better than your mother." He opened his eyes as he spoke. "I'm not going to let her take you. And Hatter won't either. But I saw no memories of what he looks like in your mind. Have you none?"

"Yes. Plenty. I try to block...how is it you can see my memories?" He grinned at her. "You cannot be my mate, Hawk. It is dangerous for you and you may die. It nearly happened to someone before."

"But he was not your mate." She wanted to believe him. Even only knowing him for less than an hour, she already liked the young shifter. "You are my mate."

She pulled away from him and was disappointed that he let her. But the moment that he stood up too, he pulled her into his arms, and she felt cherished. A feeling, she thought, she'd never felt before.

"We should dress before I lay you back down on the ground and feast on you again." Her body warmed at the thought, and he slid his hand down her body to her pussy. "Come for me this way. Let me taste you on my fingers."

Riding his fingers had her moaning loudly. She spread her legs wider for him when he slid his thigh between hers. But when he dropped down again, pulling her pussy to his mouth, she held onto his head, not sure whether it was to keep him there or to simply keep from falling. When his fingers slid into her ass again, she gripped him tighter, wanting to come so badly that she was weak from it. When his voice in her head commanded that she release, Awnia held him to her as she cried out. Cried until she was hoarse from it. When he stood up, he held her again, but his cock was digging into her hip again.

His cock was hard and the tip of it leaked his cum from the tip in a long hot stream. She wanted to taste him as he had her. Take him into her mouth and suckle him until he filled her throat with his seed. When she reached for him, he backed away. But he did wrap his hand around his cock in a way that told her that he needed relief as well.

"If you take me like you want, I'm going to come. And it will be quick and hard." Her fingers curled into his. "You know what I want to do? I want to fuck your mouth."

"Yes." She laid him back on the ground and sat between his legs. His cock stood straight up from his body, and she got her first look at him. "You're so long and hard. And thick. I love the way you fill me."

"Ride me. Please?" Shaking her head, she leaned to him and licked the cum from him. His moan encouraged her to do more, and she curled her tongue around his crown. The moment he pulled her tightly over him, she swallowed, feeling him slide past the tight muscles of her throat as he'd done to her pussy.

He did fuck her hard. It was wonderful. So when he pulled her back and nearly threw her to the ground, she wondered what she'd done wrong. But he flipped her to her belly and slammed his cock deep into her, even as he leaned over her and bit into her shoulder. The climax had her pushing back at him, at each of his strokes, as he emptied himself into her over and over. This time when she felt herself fade out, she didn't even try to fight it, she just let it settle over her as he was.

When she woke, he was sitting near her, dressed. Her nudity made her feel exposed, but when he smiled at her, it made her feel marginally better. She said nothing while she dressed in borrowed things.

"Samuel and the rest of them are at the house. I've spoken to him and he's happy for us." She didn't tell him again that they couldn't be mates. At this point she was enjoying this too much to spoil it. "He said to tell you congratulations."

"He will not think so when Hatter comes." She was angry now and not sure why. "I should think you'd be upset too. There are people at your house and we're out here playing."

"Making love." She growled at him as she tried to find her shoe. "We were not playing. However, if you'd like for me to show you the difference, I can. In fact, it would be my pleasure."

"You cannot want to have sex again." Lowering her voice, she tried again. "Men do not like sex that often. I've been with men that would only come —"

He put his hand over her mouth. "Let's not talk about other men and sex with you. I'm reasonably sure that you and Vinnie had sex." She nodded. "All right. But I don't want to hear about it. We're a couple now and we will be the only ones having sex with each other. That sounded better in my head. What I mean is, we're a couple and we will only be making love to each other."

"I understood you." He kissed her mouth and pulled back. "I'm not sure how to tell you this, again, but I've been cursed. We cannot be mates. The sex is fantastic, very much so, but we can't be mates. You have to understand that when Temptress or the Hatter come here, and they will, it will be to take me away. They mean to have my powers."

"We are a couple and to me, it matters little what they think they're going to do. We are a mated, bonded couple. Say it with me, Awnia, a mated bonded couple."

It was tempting to pick up a rock and hit him in the head with it. But he was moving along with her hand in his. By the time she could see his house, she had convinced herself that he was nuts and that she was going to miss him when they had him committed. Just before they went into the back door of his large house, he pulled her to him and kissed her.

"I can read your thoughts." When he closed her mouth for her, she wanted to bite him. "Not nice. But if you want to bite me, I can find any number of places it would feel better than where you're thinking. Although my cock really loved what you did with your mouth, I think you were meaning to hurt me."

"In order to be my mate, do you have any idea what is required of you?" He shook his head. "Then for all you know, you might have to be boiled in oil and then flayed alive."

"Boiling me in oil would not leave me very alive, that much I do know. And if you flay me...I'm not sure what would happen about me living through that. I do know that it matters little. I don't think you could hurt me anyway." He kissed her again, and she did try to bite his lip. "You're a hell cat. I cannot wait to see you tied to my bed with nothing on, but my mouth touching you for a long while. As soon as our company leaves, I'll take you to my room and show you...hell, I'll even let you show me a few things."

"Hawk, if my mother even thinks you are my mate, she will kill you before we can make sure. There are things...she cursed me to where I cannot have a mate, as I have told you like fifty times now. And to try to find out if you truly are will...I will never allow that to happen again. Once nearly took away my dearest friend." He asked her if it was Vinnie.

"Yes. He thought to be my mate and it nearly killed him. I can't let that happen to someone again. Not ever."

"I am your mate, love. I know that you don't want to believe it, but I am." She shook her head. "Whatever happens from now on will happen no matter how many times you say no. But believe me when I tell you, everyone in that room is going to know the second they smell us. We are well and truly mated." She stopped him from entering the house with her hand on his chest. She could feel his heart beating, his breaths going in and out of his lungs. She wanted to believe him. More than anything in this world. But he just didn't understand. She wouldn't let him be hurt.

"Hawk, when she comes, I won't be able to protect you from her. She has powers over me that will make it impossible for me to help you. And she will come. Sooner rather than later. And once she has me where she wants me, she'll kill me and give you to the hounds. Her hounds." He nodded, but she could see that he was trying to understand. "Hell hounds, Hawk. She has her own pair."

The door opened then and a small, compact woman pulled them both into her arms. Then she jerked them into the house so quickly that she stumbled. Awnia looked around the spacious room, then at the little couple that was bowing before her.

"You're owls." The little man looked up at her with a smile and winked. "How did you...? A faerie granted you the ability to be humans."

"She did." The woman looked as if she might want to fight her, but looked at Hawk. "You've a mate? You've...well, thank goodness! Who is she? When do we meet her?"

"Awnia, I'd like for you to meet two of the sweetest dense people I know. This is Margo Hobbs and her mate,

Deacon Hobbs. And yes, they're owls." Hawk looked at Margo. "This is my mate. Awnia Solis. She's a sun goddess, and the one we're going to protect."

"I'm sorry, my lady. I thought...there is no scent about you of him. I'm so terribly sorry." Margo bowed again, and her husband stood in front of her. "We never thought...he's like a child to us. And we thought—"

"I'm not upset. And the reason there is no scent is because...." They both looked at her. "I've been trying to tell Hawk that we're not mates. But he won't listen. He seems to think that we are. But we can't be. I can't have a mate."

"Why not?" She looked at Deacon. "If you don't mind my asking, my lady. Why can you not have a mate? Seems, if you ask me, that you've found yourself a good one. And so what if there's no scent of him on you? He is certainly carrying yours." The older man flushed and apologized.

"No harm done, I assure you. My mother will not allow it, you see. She has put a curse on me so that no one will ever love me. This curse she's put on me, it will kill anyone that tries to have me in their heart. I know that it works...I've seen it kill before. So you see, he can't be my mate or he'd be dead now. She's said so." Which was an understatement if there ever was one. Awnia noticed the loaves of bread spread out on the cutting table. She wanted a slice or two of one so badly that she had to put her hands behind her back. "I understand you're having guests for dinner. Can I help?"

They both looked at each other, then at Hawk. She had a feeling that they were terrified she'd burn everything, and for some reason, that struck her funny. She was still laughing when she was led to the living room, where some of Hawk's friends were already sitting. Hawk introduced her to the few she didn't know.

"Everyone, I'd like for you to meet my mate. Please don't get into a long boring conversation with her telling you that she's not. I'm her mate and we'll leave it at that." Awnia was hugged by them all. After, of course, they asked for permission to do so.

"I'm very glad to meet you all." She sat down on the couch next to Kennedy and Thor, a woman she'd not met until now. This pride was bigger than she'd thought, and much more diverse. She was going to enjoy these friendly people as much as she could.

CHAPTER 5

"I will not have this." Temptress looked around the room at the men bowing before her. Her men, loyal only to her. "Where is she right now?"

"We are looking, my lady." That pissed her off. The daughter was out there finding her mate and they didn't know where she was. All would be lost, everything she'd planned for would be gone, and these idiots just didn't seem to understand that at all. "There has been some confusion since the young wizard came into the picture."

Vega Pruitt. Damn him. She was sick to death of that bastard too. He'd had to have more power. Then he wanted more. After he'd found her daughter and lost her again, he'd had to heal. The man was an endless list of things he needed, and there had been very little returned to her.

"What has he done?" No one answered her, and she lifted up the closest guard with her magic. He looked terrified, and she was sure that he was going to wet himself soon. "I asked you a question. What has he done now?"

"He has tried to capture her again, but hurt her instead." The man sailed across the room. Temptress didn't want her hurt. She wanted her to suffer and die. The nerve of her mate to have singled her out of all the daughters that she had. Temptress started pacing, only to be brought up short when she heard him coming down the hall.

Halmar came into the room and only looked at the supine men before her, then the man that was broken on the floor across from them. He said nothing but snapped his fingers, and all of them, the dead man included, disappeared. Temptress hated that he had more power than her. Had she thought to make friends instead of enemies long ago, she might be better off now.

"I want you to stop this nonsense now." She tried to look innocent, but he wasn't buying it. "I wish another child of you, one that I will raise for my own, one to keep me company. You'll do it now, today. And you will break this curse you have on the children you have with me. I wish for her, my child, to be happy. With a man she can love and be loved by. This man she's to be mated to, he'll be a good man, and should be — "

"You know of him?" Her face flushed with anger, and she wanted to go to a mirror and see if it had caused her any damage. But this...right now, this was more important. "I will not break my curses on her. Awnia should never have been allowed to live any more than the rest of them were."

The moment it left her mouth, she knew her mistake. All this time she knew that he thought the children she'd had, all of them, had died at birth...or in Awnia's case, as a teenager. Now he knew, if the look on his face was any indication. The thunder of his anger shook her room, tore pictures from the walls, and set doors off their hinges. No one would come to her aid, she knew this. Temptress had made too many people jealous of her beauty and intelligence in her life with him.

He had her up off the floor with his hand around her throat so quickly that she lashed out at him before she could think how bad an idea that really was. Her body, like that of the man she'd thrown, hit the wall hard. But when she hit it, she shattered the wall behind her rather than her skull. Temptress hurt so badly, and lay there stunned for too long before she realized she should have run.

As he came at her, Halmar was speaking a language that she'd never heard before. It occurred to her that other than the few hundred times they'd had sex, she rarely spent any time with him. Which, she supposed, was best, since they hated each other with a great deal of passion.

"Where is my daughter? Where are the others?" She didn't have a clue what he was asking her, but before she could ask him, he asked her in that barely controlled, angered voice, "Where are my other children? I'm assuming there were more than just Awnia."

"Well of course there were. It was our curse, was it not?" He told her it was her curse. "Semantics. You were cursed as well. You do have to sleep with me once a year. And there was an issue each time. As for where they are? I have no clue. Nor do I care."

"You cold, heartless, fucking cunt." Temptress shrugged. "Where did you have them taken? And which minions did you have do your dirty work? I shall kill them all."

"None of them would help me, you know that. You turned everyone against me with your lies and hatred." She didn't want to tell him what she'd done with the brats. She knew as surely as he was standing there that he'd hurt her for it. "Are you here to fuck me? Because if you are, then let's get this over with. I have much more important things to do than wait for you to get your rocks off."

He shivered. "Never again. Never shall I touch you." Temptress perked up. If he didn't come to her bed, then she could— "No other man shall either. I'll put...since you are so fond of curses, then I'll tell you that there is one attached to you. So long as you are in this world, no person will ever want to have sex with you again."

Her body felt as if he'd blown her up. She was tossed back so quickly that she was sure if she was facing the wall, she'd be dead...well, as dead as one of their kind could be. But when she landed, her body slamming against something profoundly hard, she lay there trying to take an accounting of her body. Everything was broken, but to what extent she couldn't tell. The room was darker, it seemed, than black.

"Are you still living, Temptress?" She didn't answer Halmar. His voice echoed through what she thought was a small structure. "Too bad really. You're not going to enjoy where you are. The pit I've been saving just for you for a good many decades. And do you know what else I've done?"

The blinding light took her breath away, and she had to shield her face with her hands. The pain made her cry out. Halmar laughed from what she could now see was a long, deep tunnel that was as dark as the light was bright. His figure, large and imposing when he was near her, was a small dot from where she was now. The light, now that she could see it, was shining on a single item, a small round mirror. As her body began to heal, she made her way to it and wasn't surprised to see that it was marred with cracks. But the face reflected back at her couldn't have been hers.

"What's the meaning of this? You cannot do this to me. I am your wife. We have a contract, you and I. I demand that you bring me out of here this minute. I'm not kidding, Halmar. Get me out of here." He laughed harder. "And whose face is this that you torment me with? Our daughter's? I knew she was going to be ugly as soon as she was pulled from my body. Why do you even care where the brat is? She's nothing. I want out of here."

"Nay, you'll not be taken from there any time soon. And it is not her that I show you, Temptress the bitch. Though when I find her, I will give you an image of her to haunt you. That is you that looks back at you from the mirror." Temptress looked in the mirror again and wanted to argue with him. "It is. You look that way without your magic. I've taken it from you as well. At least the magic you thought you needed for your beauty. And now that I see what your true self looks like, I'm wholly glad that you used it. Christ, you are one ugly fucking bitch."

"Take me out of here. Now, Halmar. I will not stand for this." The pinpoint of light where he stood disappeared with a loud bang. But the small light on the mirror stayed. And no matter how hard she tried, Temptress could not see beyond it into the room. "Halmar? You've had your fun. Take me out of here now and I'll give you the next child. Halmar?"

~~~

Temptress had no concept of time, but it seemed as if it had been forever since anyone had come to see her. She was sure that only a few hours had passed, but it seemed as if it had been days. Food had appeared on her lap twice now. And in that time, little or not, she'd had plenty of time to think and plan. She was going to kill his fucking ass as soon as she took care of the daughter. No one treated her this way and got away with it.

She was tempted to call on her servant. But she suspected that if she did that, she'd have maybe a single time with her and nothing more. So she worked out what she wanted her to do and how to do it. Rysdan had been with her for only the last two decades or so, but she'd proven herself invaluable in that short amount of time. The girl possessed some magical talent, but not anything like Temptress had. But her one talent was going to get Temptress out of there and to the realm that the daughter was in.

When she was finished, covering all her angles and all the things that could go wrong, Temptress looked into the mirror again. The hideous face that stared back at her made her close her eyes for just a moment before she looked again.

"Halmar, you're going to pay for this. See if you don't. And so will that brat of yours. Awnia will never be an issue for me again." Calling to Rysdan, she thought for sure that Halmar had taken that from her as well. But when she appeared in her mirror, Temptress was thrilled.

"My lady." Rysdan would never say a word about her looks. She'd seen her as very few had over the years, but only looked down when she told her she needed her. "You've only to ask, my lady."

"Good. I have a long list of things I need for you to do. And in a specific order. You should write this down." As she went to get pen and paper, Temptress smiled. This was going to be the best plan she'd ever had.

~~~

"You have to have a reason for this...what you believe is a good reason at any rate. I'd like to hear it." Hawk sat down at his table and waited for Awnia to do the same. Two faeries had come to stay with him as soon as he'd purchased the house, and they sat on the little cotton ball that Margo had laid out for them. They sat before she did. "Sit down and tell me please. I'd like to have a better understanding."

Awnia sat, but she didn't look like she'd be there for long. Margo set a cup of tea in front of her, then a plate of cookies. He noticed that there was a large pile of crumbs to one side of the plate, and wasn't surprised when the two little faeries went to it and picked up several pieces.

"They belong to you now?" Hawk nodded at Awnia when she asked about Nelena and Serane, who had volunteered to be his house faeries. "Vinnie has always had a great relationship with them as well. Once when I was just new to this earth, he had them make me a dress to wear. It was...different than anything I'd ever worn before. I felt human for a time. Then he took me to dinner, and the only thing I had to wear was the clothing I had on when I was dropped here. Not even it was in very good shape."

"Dropped?" She nodded and looked at him. "You mean that someone literally dropped you here? Where from, if I may ask?"

"Above." She didn't go into any more detail, and Hawk was sort of glad for that. He had no idea where above might be, but for now, that was enough. "My mother's name is Temptress. Have you heard of her?"

"No. Should I have?" Awnia laughed and told him Temptress would certainly think he should. "And your father, I'm assuming he's a god, too."

"Yes. Temptress is a beauty, or so she makes everyone believe with her magic. Halmar, my father, is a maker. As to what he makes, it would depend on what the other gods, the stronger gods, need from him. He is powerful and full of magic. But he was cursed; not as I was, but worse in that he had to marry Temptress." He asked her why. "When he was a younger man, he was in love with Temptress and she him, I suppose. Not with her, the witch told him, but with the beauty that she let everyone think she had. It...he was mesmerized by her, I suppose. And he was stupid with his claim to have her, he told me later. He claimed that her beauty would fade. It was the woman he wanted. And no matter how many times the witch told him that his love was not his own, he would not believe her. Then one day, he took Temptress to his bed. She'd been meant for another, and instead of killing him, which was well within his rights as a cockled man, the other man thanked Halmar and asked that he only be cursed."

"So he raped her." Awnia shook her head. "Ah, so she wanted him just as badly. And so they were put together as punishment."

"No. She was willing because she thought Halmar could give her things that the other man could not. I was never sure as to what that might have been, but after they were wed, it came out that he didn't have this power or whatever she wanted. It was said then that the marriage became one of war. And each time they had sex, there would be an issue. The first child, a boy child, died within minutes of his birth. The witch said that too much magic had been used by the mother to keep him well enough to survive the natural world around him. Halmar was mad with the pain of losing his child. He cursed at the witch and Temptress. But neither woman cared, it seemed, enough to suit him. The witch knew it was his grief, and Temptress was already planning." With a wave of her hand, a hologram of two people appeared above the table. "This is them. My parents. It is thought that for many, many years my mother would not conceive, that her magic and the power of her domain kept her from having an issue. But there were. Each time that there was a child born to her, she would…she tossed them to this realm."

Hawk watched in horror as the woman moved to the edge of a large opening in her floor and dropped the still screaming child into it. He didn't have to know that the baby wouldn't survive such a fall, and when Awnia continued, she explained to him while he was speechless at just how helpless the child really had been.

"Until an issue, a child, is ten and six, they are not magical. They have nothing more than a child born of any human here on this earth. Any magic that there would be was gifted to them by the witch. But she can only give them so much. What she is said to have done was pull some from each of the parents and make it stronger. Mine was the sun. And as my sires were lower gods, I too became a goddess then as well." As he watched the hologram, it changed into a child kneeling before a woman in many robes, a colorful robe that hid her face and body from him. She touched the child on the forehead, and she glowed for a moment before her eyes changed to a shade of blue so intense that it was hard to see. Then it faded out to the color that Awnia's were now...still very blue, but not glowing. He wondered for a moment if it was her when the image changed again. This child was sickly, in a bed covered in blankets with a fire roaring in the background. He knew that this was his Awnia, and that the witch was giving her whatever she needed.

"Is that why you survived? Because she came to you even though you were dying?" He knew that he wasn't going to like the answer when she smiled sadly at him and nodded. "She's not going to get you. And this curse that she's done to you, it will be broken."

"On the day that I was born, my father saved me. As I was being prepared by Temptress for my final journey, he happened upon her and took me to his chambers before I was tossed away like so many before me. I wasn't supposed to learn of this, but I found her once. Temptress was tossing a small bundle through the opening, and I knew somehow what she was doing wasn't right. It wasn't until years later that I knew why. There were many more after, I would imagine. Once I was with Halmar, he protected me. I knew, even as a small child, that what he was doing was unheard of. A man, a god like him, caring for his issue. But he did. And for many years, it was just the two of us." The scene changed before him and there stood the same man teaching his daughter to use a bow and arrow. Then another of him teaching her to swim. As Hawk watched, the child became a teenager, until the scenes stopped altogether.

"I was too pretty, she said." The woman appeared, her face contorted in anger. She was shaking the girl child hard, and Hawk felt his body scream at him to take action. "Her curse was not just to have a child a year, but to have them until one child would exceed her beauty. That child would bring her heartache, so much so that Temptress would know pain as she'd never felt before. And that child would rule in her place."

"Rule what?" Hawk reached over and took Awnia's hand and held it tightly within his. When she looked at him, her eyes filled with tears, he reached over and picked her up and sat her on his lap. "Rule what?"

"The kingdom in which they live. All of it." He held her tightly as she cried. He hurt for her, but knew that when she told him everything, he was going to protect her, protect her as well as he could for just being a shifter. "She will destroy you and all that are in your heart. It was what she said to me when she told me there would be no love for me. She said that to me just before I took ill. I never...something happened to me then that I've never been sure of, but I was tossed here. Only because of the fact that the witch gave me my magic as I lay there was I able to be here now. Temptress told me that any man stupid enough to love and love all of me, she would tear apart, along with all that were in his heart. And she will too, if she finds out about you."

Hawk held her as she cried. It tore him up inside to hear her, and his heart broke for the burden that she'd been carrying. As she quieted down, he looked at Margo. She'd been there the entire time, and he'd completely forgotten about her, as well as the little faeries. When Hawk was sure Awnia was asleep, he spoke to his dear friend.

"I don't know what to do." She nodded and held her hand to her heart. "I have to protect her. I have to…I'm in love with her."

"Of course you are. And why not? But she's not in a good place. We have to think. Let me…." She looked at the little faeries. "Do you think you can find us someone to speak to? Someone that will be able to talk to this Halmar?"

Nelena looked at Serane before nodding. "It is said that our Yve has a connection to the gods. We…it is why we are so in awe of her. She is very special. We have never seen it, but we have heard of it." Hawk watched as the two little ones spoke amongst themselves before looking at him. "We will go to her now, but we feel there will be a need for her to have more magic around her. May we call in help?"

"I want you to do whatever you deem necessary to keep her safe."

He should have said within reason. He knew that they were literal in their thinking, but before he could clarify, before he could say, "Let me revise that," there were so many faeries in his kitchen that he felt his vision blur with them. When Awnia was taken from his arms, he thought to fight them, but there were too many of them. As they moved from this room to the next he stood up, but suddenly Yve, one of the faeries from Vinnie's, was there. She sat down on the plate with the cookies still on it and picked at it until she had several crumbs. When she seemed satisfied with her selection, she turned and looked at him with a smile.

"What I am about to tell you is a held secret. You must never tell anyone, living or dead, please. I have contact with the faeries of her world. I have had for a long while." Hawk leaned forward in his chair, as did Margo. Hawk nodded for her to go on. "Halmar is…his temper is not the best, and he is angered now. I do not know the reason, but I cannot approach him at the moment. But there is another I can talk to."

"I understand. Can I?" She shook her head at him. "Does he know that she's in trouble? That her mother is going to kill her?"

"He thinks her dead, as does the rest of the kingdom. His grief was profound, and still hurts him a great deal." Hawk had thought that might be why he'd never come to her. "She was ill, very ill for a time. Just before her coming of age, she had been poisoned. There was never proof of how she had gotten the poison, but it still entered her body. The witch was at her side at all times during this illness, but it was…her body, Awnia's body, disappeared from the castle. No one knew where she'd gone, and the witch disappeared soon after. It was believed for a long time that Temptress killed her. But there was no proof. When there were no more children born of the god and goddess, it was assumed that the witch had been the one to hold the curse. Now…we faeries are not sure now."

"I am sure that the witch held the magic." The big shifter, Big Will, appeared in the kitchen. Margo simply got up and pulled the rolls she'd been working on for him out of the refrigerator and began to work on them. "I have spoken to her. She is not of this world or the other, but she is very happy that the young princess lives."

"She is dead then? The witch is dead?" Big Will nodded. "No one knew that she was alive all this time? That she was out there alone? How is that possible?"

"Magic." As if that should explain it all, Hawk thought sourly, and started to ask Big Will to explain when Yve did.

"Vinnie and she were friends for many years, more than most any of us have been here. He knew that she was a goddess, but not her story. It was not until Halmar put out the word that he looks for her, his child, that anyone began to look for her. We looked for many years, it is told, but I think that everyone assumed, like they did in the other realm, that she had not survived. And now...we have not...no one is telling Lord Halmar anything for fear of Temptress." Hawk could understand that. He'd seen her rage at just having a child. "We can go to him, to the god, but it will cost you."

"Whatever it takes." Yve nodded and smiled at him. "I'm guessing you think I should have asked what it would cost. But to be honest with you, I'd pay with my life if that is what it would take to save her. She needs to...I want her to be happy. She's not. And I don't think she has been for a very long time."

"It is doubtful, my lord, that he would ask you to surrender your life, but Temptress may. And it is doubtful that she would bother to ask." He nodded. "I shall have the other faeries watch over her. They will abide by the same rules that they do at the other houses, correct?"

"Yes, please." Hawk had no idea what those rules might be, but if the rest of the pride was okay with them, then he could be as well. "I'm not sure how this works. I know that the two that have been here for several days...I'm assuming that they'll be the ones in charge, so to speak."

"Yes, my lord, Nelena and Serane will keep the others in line. If they need help, I'll come to help them, but I doubt they will." He nodded. "They will rule the house to a point. The other faeries will come to them with questions, and they will...Margo and Deacon will keep them in line. As fellow shifters, they will know what you require."

"Yes. They'll know everything." Hawk looked at the closed door that Awnia had been carried out of. "I'm in love with her. I never thought it would happen, but now that she's in my life, I can't think how I managed all this time without her."

"As it should be." He turned and looked at Yve when she said his name. "If Halmar is able to free her, you will no longer be able to live in this realm, my lord. She is a great queen, and will need to be with her kind."

"She'll do what she wants. I'll be at her side for anything she needs of me." Yve nodded, but looked as if she might say more. "Please contact her father for me. Tell him that I can't protect her on my own. Not with the odds I've seen."

"I will, my lord."

As soon as she left him, Hawk looked at his friend, Big Will. He had not aged a second, it seemed, in the five or so years since he'd seen him last.

"I will stay as well. There are things about that I can do?" Hawk nodded. "And Margo will not mind feeding me?"

She hit him in the back of the head and told him to behave. Few would have done such a thing to him and gotten away with it. But Margo had sort of adopted the man when he'd been on a visit with him years and years ago.

Their relationship was one formed of a deep mutual love and understanding that few, himself included, would or could understand.

"I have already got your room ready for you. Things that I know you like are there as well." He thanked her. When Big Will and he had set up a schedule for each of them to take turns watching the perimeter, Hawk went to find Awnia.

She was lying on the bed, covered by a light blanket, when he entered the room. There were faeries in the room — the ceiling was covered in them — but as soon as he sat on the bed, all but two left.

"I wish to be alone with her."

Nodding, they too left, but he knew that they'd be close. Lying down next to her, he was pleased when Awnia wrapped her body around his and held him. Hawk was exhausted from all this emotional upheaval and stress and closed his eyes. He knew that he had to keep alert, but right now all he could think of was that she was in trouble. Just as he was about to let himself drift off, a ghost of considerable age, his friend, came to him in his ghostly form.

"I have eyes on Vega. You'll be happy to know that he's in a bit of a bind himself." Hawk asked him in what way. "The mark on his face makes it difficult for him to go unnoticed. Did you do that? Matters little, he is marked by someone. And even to go into the smallest of stores, someone stares. I will keep tabs on him for you and the girl. She is very lovely, by the way."

"She is." Hawk asked him if he needed anything else, anything at all. Mandel told him that he had it under control and would speak to him as Vega moved. "Thank you."

As the being, a ghost he'd rescued from a car a long time ago, disappeared, Hawk relaxed. Mandel was a young man full of himself and what he thought he could do as a ghost. Many times in all the years he'd been hanging around Hawk, he'd told him a great many things he'd done, none of which were true. But his heart was in the right place and Hawk thought him a good kid. And he knew as surely as he lay there that he would do as he'd said he would. If Vega so much as caught a cold, Mandel would tell Hawk immediately.

CHAPTER 6

Halmar moved among the humans as a spectrum. He could not come to this place as a real being for fear of Temptress finding out. If she found him here, she'd know that his daughter was close and may be able to harm the child before he could save her.

To be honest, he didn't care overly much for humans enough to want to spend too much time with them, but he knew from others that Awnia might be here. And right now, he'd do just about anything to find her, even hang with the nasty mortals. But his child was here, his little Awnia, and he needed to see her.

For the most part, they were loud and had opinions of themselves that far outreached what they really were. They had an odor about them...something akin to old meat that had been lying in the sun too long. Although it had been some decades since he'd been here, these people still had an odor about them, but it was not nearly as bad.

Two days ago, a faerie had come to see him. In his mood—well, his current mood too, if he was honest with himself—he'd had her sent away. No one had bothered to get her name or where she was from. Had it not been for the fact that this faerie had smelled of human and dragon, he might not have been able to find out just which realm she'd been from.

As a small brownie made his way to him, Halmar stepped back into an alley and waited.

"We have word of five dragons in this realm, my worship. One is very old and has had no contact with a human for many years." Halmar told him that wasn't who he wanted. "There are two pairs of them. One pair is a common enough type, but their blood is so weak with their former self that it is doubtful that they know who they are. We have reason to believe that they have never shifted in their life, but that they are together shows that there is just enough magic within them to bring them together. And they have no children."

"You mean they don't know that they're dragon?" The brownie nodded, his face looking pleased that Halmar would understand such a thing. "That is very sad. To be something so amazing and to not know it. Sad indeed. And the other pair? What of them?"

"The male is a great dragon, a blue one. Rare even by our standards, my lord." Halmar had two dragons of his own, but neither were blue. "The other, my lord, is a golden one. And sir, she is breeding."

Halmar felt his shock. A golden dragon? They had been gone for so long that he'd not seen...well, he couldn't remember when he'd last seen one. He asked where they were, thinking that a blue and golden dragon would surely have a faerie, such as the one that had been to see him.

"Not ten miles from here, my lord. The female is breeding, as I said, so they are to the skies more than they are not. You know how the female can be during such a time. But, my lord, you will need to know that they are members of a strong pride. And this pride is well known to all of us here on this earth. The leader is a man of great worth." Halmar tried to think what a pride was, and then it occurred to him.

"A pride is not a group of dragons, brownie. They are called a cemetery. A pride is how one would refer to a group of cats." The brownie nodded. "I don't understand you. Are you saying that they now call themselves a pride?"

"Oh no, my lord, they are the two of them and they are…this pair belongs to a pride, a pride of cats. Lions to be exact. The male that runs it is a good man, as I have said. His pride has a great many shifters. His mate is reputed to be one of kindness and goodness, but also fierce and protective." This was getting stranger and stranger all the time. Then the brownie spoke again. "The pride is not like any other. There is a wolf, a bear, and a vampire as well. The man that we seek, the dragon, is there with a shifter. And not just a shifter, my lord, but an elite one. One that is said to talk to the dead."

Strange indeed. He knew that there were bands of this kind of shifters. They would be lonely and seek out others of their ilk, whether it be like themselves or simply others for a time. But to stay together, to live together, as this brownie was implying, was odd indeed.

"I shall talk to him, this shifter. He will be my way to the pride. I have…he and I will have much in common, and I will talk to him tonight about the dragon and his faerie." The brownie nodded and left him with the man's name. It would be all he needed to speak to the man through his magic.

Halmar needed to be home to speak to the shifter, and willed himself to his home and his room. As soon as he was in his chamber, he reached out for the shifter. He was surprised to find the man at rest, and his opinion of him lowered somewhat. To be a slob during this time of day was not something that Halmar tolerated well.

You will speak to me. Halmar had a thought that he should be gentler when talking with the man, but he was in a hurry. He could only keep Temptress in the pit for so long before she got out. The subjects were more loyal to him, of course, but they were terrified of her. *Wake up and speak to me.*

The man let him into his mind, but only so far. That impressed Halmar, but he didn't let the man know. To be able to keep him from his thoughts, the man was strong indeed.

Who the hell are you and what the fuck do you want? If you belong to the table downstairs, I'm not in the mood at the moment to talk to you. Can you not see that there are other things going on that —?

I wish you to shut up and listen to me. You know a dragon. I would like to know if he has a faerie with him of great strength. There was no answer but for the man to search his mind. Halmar felt his gentle search and let the man, like he had done, go only so far. But when he pushed past the first barrier he'd put up, Halmar had to work hard to put up another, then another. *You will stop this now.*

You're a god. Halmar, if I'm not mistaken. Halmar was taken aback by the humor in the man's voice. *Yve works faster than I thought. What is it you can help me with? I'm working on a plan to keep her safe now, and —*

Me help you? I'm here for you to help me. I wish to speak to this dragon. He is a blue one and his mate golden. There was a faerie to see me, but I sent her away before I could —

Don't you care about your daughter? Awnia? Halmar willed his mind to look deeply into the man's. And when he saw her, his little Awnia, his spectral image dropped to his knees beside their bed. The man only watched him, for which Halmar was very grateful.

It is her. The man moved off the bed but stood beside it. *She is really here? Alive? May I speak to her?*

No, I don't think that's a good idea. I have a feeling...and this is just a feeling on my part, but I would bet there are people watching you. The man stood between him and his child, and Halmar stood up. *Let's take this to the living room so she can rest. She's had a really hard few days.*

Halmar looked at her. She did look unwell. Not sick, because she couldn't become ill...at least he didn't think so. But she did look tired. He looked at the man who still stood there.

I didn't know she lived. They told me...that bitch told me that she was dead.

The man nodded and then nodded to the door. Halmar started to point out to the man that he was no more there than the man was in the castle with him, but moved to the door. When it was opened, he stood in the hallway as if he were there and waited on the man until he exited. "I should explain to you what I am doing here."

"If the bitch, as you called her, is moving to come here, then I get it. I want to protect Awnia as much as you do, if not more. But I'm only a shifter, and that...well, as she's my mate, it's my duty to seek help—"

"Mate?" The man nodded. "She knows. The lying cunt knows then. She said that. When I went to see what was going on with her, she said, 'then you know of him,' or something like that." They were at the bottom of the stairs now and moved into a large airy room. Halmar thought he could enjoy this room, and pretended to move to stand near the empty grate. The man laughed as he sat down.

"I guess you're not really here. Are you?" The man was very smart, very smart indeed. Halmar told him he wasn't. "So you not being here, it's not going to help us overly much. I was hoping somehow that you'd have something...I have no idea what I thought, but I assumed that you could be of some help. She's very afraid, and we're not really sure how to keep her safe against a goddess. And she will come here, won't she?"

"Yes. If I don't miss my bet, she's more than likely making plans to come here now. I would say that...I would say that she's an evil bitch that will do her damnedest to harm you both and to take Awnia away from you. And me. But I won't let her do that. I can't let her do that. I will help you as much as you need me." Halmar looked at the man, then at the ceiling above them. "I cannot believe that she's here with you. Safe. And you're her mate, you say?"

"Yes. She keeps telling me that I'm not, but I assure you that I am." Halmar frowned, but the man continued before he could ask him why she thought that. "She's worried that, as you've said, her mother will kill us both. Awnia said that she threatened her with that just before she was taken ill."

"That does sound like...I'm very sorry. I'm Halmar. I don't think I got your name." He told him. "Hawk, what a strong name. And this is your animal to call, this hawk? And I heard that you speak with the dead."

"Not just the human dead, but anyone. I speak with all sorts of things. Whenever anyone needs me, I can talk to them. Sometimes it takes a little on my part to get them to open up, but we get there eventually." He stood up and walked to a little book. "This has the spirit of the woman who wrote in it every day. She passed some years later, alone and lonely. I talk to her sometimes. She gives me a glimpse into the past like no one else can." He picked up another item after laying the book aside. "But this is a knife that called to me. Not the person who used it, but the knife itself. He was also lonely, he said, and only wanted someone to talk to him. There are times when his tales are too much for me to listen to, but I do. For him."

"We have a word for what you can do. Kiarain. It means people of the soul. Not necessarily of a person, but of anything. We believe that everything is alive." Hawk nodded. "It's a gift that few have, and fewer still will use. I'm very impressed with you, young Hawk. But something does bother me. You said that my Awnia said you are not her mate. Why does she say this, do you know?"

"I think it's more of fear." Halmar nodded but said nothing else. There had to be a reason for her to not have given him what he needed. And until he talked with her, Halmar wasn't going to mention their bonding process. "This curse that Temptress put on her. Can you tell me why a woman would do that to her own daughter? Awnia has shown me parts of her life with her…I really hate to call her mother, but I suppose that's what she is to her. But to do this to your own child? How is that…why?"

"I wish I knew. I know that she is a horrible person. I wish…was it not for the fact that I do have my daughter, I would say that I wish I had never met Temptress. I was duped from the very beginning. Not that I wasn't warned, but I still messed up terribly. To think…there were so many young lives taken by her. She killed them, you know? All the children that we could have raised together. Small, innocent lives that she cut so short without a single shred of mercy or compassion." Hawk nodded. "You know about this? Awnia, she told you? You know how Temptress did this monstrous act?"

"She tossed them out of a hole in her room. They were still…the two that I saw were still covered in their birth."

Though he wasn't there in the room with him, Halmar reached for the chair. His hand passed through it, and he had to stagger back to his own bed in his own room. He could hear Hawk shouting for him, but he could no longer move. This was worse than he'd ever thought it was. Far worse.

"I am…I'm not fine, but I'm…I don't know what I am." Hawk walked in front of him but didn't say anything. "I never knew. I didn't even know there were other children born alive but my Awnia. And to think that she murdered them without…. She gave herself away that day by a small slip of the tongue or I might not have ever known. I thought they might have been taken away. But to have tossed them so far." Halmar looked around his room, not the one that the man still resided in. Of all the things he'd collected over his life, none of it held any value for him like his daughter did. He did have the things he treasured most, and that was the wall to his daughter. He'd put it there so that he could see it the first thing when he woke and the last thing when he closed his eyes at night.

He told Hawk that he'd get back to him. That he must think. But what he really needed was to grieve. Grieve for all the untold children that Temptress had killed. All his children, all of them that had been so heartlessly thrown away. Lying back on the bed after severing the connection, he wanted to curl into himself and die too. But he knew that Awnia needed him more than ever now.

~~~

Vega watched the scene in front of him. It held his interest but not very well. He loved porn. What man who was honest didn't? But his dick, his toy, had lost its ability to get hard long ago. Reaching down, he stroked the soft member and it didn't even stir. Looking up at the window in front of him again, he stared at the man as he tied the woman to the wall.

"What are they doing?" The woman in the room startled him, and her nudity had him looking at his locked door. "I have been watching them for a while, and I cannot figure out why she does not take her own pleasure. I would have several times by now."

"She's not allowed. It's the way they...who the hell are you?" She didn't turn from looking at the couple. The man there was eating the woman's pussy, and Vega watched as his woman slid her fingers to her own. "What do you think you're doing here?"

"I've come to talk to you. My name is Rysdan. Can you do that to me? Eat me?" She turned then, and he got a look at her entire body. Vega swallowed hard twice as he took in the vision before him. "Eat me. Then we can talk. But watching them has gotten me horny, and it's been a while since I've been fucked."

He was down on his knees in front of her before he could think. When she pressed his head to her pussy, Vega moaned at her scent. Then he took his first taste of her, and he knew that he had to have it all. Lapping at her clit over and over, he drank greedily at her. He held her as still as he could. It was hard to suckle at her because of how vigorously she was riding his mouth, but he knew that when she came, he was going to have a feast he'd not enjoyed for a very long time.

"More." He looked up at her, never taking his mouth from her. "More. I need more from you. Give it to me. Make me come over and over."

Vega slid his fingers into her pussy and with his other hand he punched through the tight barrier of her ass. Her scream when she came had him eating at her faster, actually chewing on her lips as she flooded his mouth with her cream. Vega tried his best not to miss a drop of the nectar she gave him, but Christ, she was dripping down her legs she was so wet.

"That, I need that." She had stepped back from him, and he reached for her again. Instead of letting him eat her, she turned his head to the window again. "Let me do that. Your cock is what I need now. Give it to me. I'll give you a gift if you give me what I want."

At some point the couple in the bedroom had changed. The bound woman was now loose, but the man was tied down, and his thick cock was straining from his body while she bobbed up and down on him with her mouth. But before he could tell Rysdan that he wasn't able to help her with that, the woman made her way up the man's body again. When she took his cock into her pussy, she cried out loudly. So loudly that it was audible to them on the other side of the window. And this time she was riding the inert man as hard as she could.

"Lie down." He looked at the couple, then at her. "Lie down. I need you to let me do that to you. I know it's called riding—we do it when my friend is around, but I think with you, it will be much better. Please, lie down for me."

"I can't. I'm not able to perform." She looked down at him and so did he. "I can no longer get stiff enough to fuck you, much less you ride me. Too much magic, I guess."

It was a joke. A poor one, but a joke. When she bent at the waist and wrapped her hand around him, Vega nearly came up off the floor. His cock thickened in her hand. It had been so long since he'd been hard, he watched in fascination as his cock not only lengthened and hardened, but seemed to be much bigger than he'd ever been before.

"Christ, what did you do?" He nearly came when she tightened her hand around him to the point of pain. As he stood up, with her still squeezing him, he fell back against the bed that was suddenly in the room with them. Vega reached down and wrapped his hand around himself, loving the heat of his cock, the way it seemed to beg to be inside of the beautiful woman. And Christ, he really wanted to be inside of her.

"I will take you into me now. Then I will ride you hard." He nodded as she slid up his body. Vega was so excited to be having sex again, he didn't care what she did to him. But the moment she rolled her hips over him, taking his cock into her hot wet sheath, he grabbed her hips to hang on. His balls curled up against his body, and he felt them fill.

Her ride was erratic. Finally, when she seemed to be frustrated, he pulled her hips slowly back and forth until she began to get a rhythm. Sitting up, he took her nipple into his mouth and nibbled on it gently. Then he bit her hard enough to have her cry out. But her pussy tightened around him, giving him the idea that she was enjoying it. As soon as she held him to her breast, begging him to bite her again, Vega pressed his fingers, three of them this time, into her ass and rolled her to her back.

"I have a friend that likes to eat me. She eats my pussy all the time while I eat hers. Would you like that? To eat two pussies at one time?" Vega looked at her face to see if she was kidding him as he fucked her harder. "We eat each other every night before we sleep."

"Yes, I'd like to see that." He thought about watching two women fucking each other, and he started hitting her as hard as he could, moving her body up the bed until they were at the headboard with their heads banging it.

It was a fantasy of Vega's to see two women having sex. When the bed shifted behind him, Vega turned to see another naked woman on the bed with them. This one was dark where Rysdan was light. Her long hair hung down her back in a tight braid, and all Vega wanted to do was fuck her ass while he held her hair tightly in his hand. As he was laid back, all he could think of was two women, and he was fucking hard as stone.

The second woman crawled over him. Her pussy was at his mouth when she leaned over his body to Rysdan's pussy. Vega pulled her to his mouth and began eating her shaved pussy as she ate at Rysdan's. Christ, he nearly came when she started to ride his mouth. His cock was buried deeply in Rysdan's again while he ate hungrily at the other woman. Vega was in pussy heaven.

When Rysdan cried out that she was coming, the woman at his mouth rode him harder. As she flooded his mouth with her juices as she, too, came, Vega had a thought that he should be coming as well. But the woman at his mouth moved then, and he watched as the two of them licked his cock clean of juices as they played with each other's pussies. His cock leaked more and more as they each took turns sucking him, and he needed to come. He hurt with the need to release.

"I need to come. In one of you or a mouth, but I need to come or I'm going to hurt." Rysdan looked up at him as she kissed the other woman and fisted his cock. It wasn't enough, not nearly enough for him to release. "Please. I ache to come. Help me."

As they moved over his body again, both their mouths seemed to be all over his cock. Pussies were in his mouth over and over as they took turns riding his mouth and tongue. Even his balls were being suckled as his body seemed to tense up for release. As soon as one of them gave his nuts a hard twist, Vega erupted. His cum shot so hard from his cock that it splashed him in the face. And they were right there licking him clean again and sucking him dry.

He couldn't move. Vega lay there, his heart still pounding and his breathing painfully harsh as it expelled from his lungs. But the women weren't finished with him. Nor was his cock, it seemed, ready to quit either. He was hard still, and painfully so. He wanted to stand up and jerk off, fist his cock over and over until he was empty of the pent-up orgasms that he'd held for so long. But they tossed him back to the bed, and while he ate Rysdan's pussy this time, the other woman rode his cock like a true cowgirl.

For hours the two of them fucked him, sucked him, and did everything imaginable to his poor body. When he begged them they would allow him to come, but the relief was short lived and he was hard almost as soon as he ejaculated. His balls were sore from their teeth and hands, his cock raw from being ridden like a horse, and his mouth, his lips, were aching from eating them so often. And begging them didn't stop them. Telling them that he needed a break didn't matter either. They were having their fun and he was going to give it to them.

"I'm exhausted." The girl grinned at him as she rode his cock. He'd come once more since they'd taken him, this time his cum spraying them both as he held his cock for them. He'd watched them then, his cock still stiff as they ate each other, licking his cum off their supple bodies as they moaned.

Rysdan was at his balls, sucking them while she played with his asshole. He'd been fucked there too, he knew. One of them had produced a dildo that each wore at one point, and they'd used it on him and each other several times. He'd enjoyed it a great deal, but now…he wasn't sure, but he thought they might have broken him somehow.

"Please. I need to stop this. I'm not used to having this much sex." He put his hand around her hips as she rode him. "You have to stop. I've had enough for now."

Said no man ever, he thought to himself. But as she threw back her head and shouted out her release, his own burned from the lack of release. He wanted to come again. He needed to empty again, but was too sore to have them play while he came. He lay there knowing that as soon as she shifted off him, Rysdan would take her turn. He was almost willing to bet they were trying to kill him. When nothing more happened to him, he looked down his body to see Rysdan sitting in a chair that had not been there before.

"We have enjoyed you very much. But you're right, we have work to do. And my lady will be most unhappy if we play all the time and not do as she asked of me." He looked for the other woman and only just realized she was gone. "I've sent her home. She will tell all about the fun day we had with you. You will be famous. But fun, like all things, must end. I've come to see you for a reason."

"Is that it? Is that why you're here? I know you did something to me when you touched my cock. I told you I've not been hard for a while, so you did something to me so that you could be fucked by me. And while I enjoy what you did for me, that was a little much for any man. Men, even men of great magic as I have, will need to rest after something like that." She grinned at him and he saw the fangs. "What are you?"

"I am the servant to the goddess Temptress. Have you heard of her?" He nodded. "She said that you had. But I wanted to make sure. She would like to know where you are with the daughter. She wants her now. My lady is hoping to get this thing with her completed before much longer."

"I've lost her." Rysdan nodded and stood up. She was clothed now, and he felt decidedly embarrassed to still be hard and naked too. He glanced down at his cock and moaned in pain when he touched the raw tip to wipe away a drop of cum. "Will I continue to be hard like this? Forever?"

"Would you like to be?" He would like to have an erection once in a while, but not hard all the time. He told her that. "You will have to explain to me when you would like this to occur. I could have sex always, and I do when it suits me. Men should be more like that. Just have sex when it pleases you. Or not. It would be good for me if you were not in the mood, as you are now, that I could take as much pleasure as I wish and not bother with you having to be in the mood as well."

"It doesn't work that way, sadly. And if you see what you've done to me, it will be obvious to you that my body can't handle that sort of thing either. We usually only are able to come once or twice, but not as many times as I have today." She nodded but didn't say anything. "What was with the marathon of sex? Not that I didn't enjoy it, but you didn't come here for that."

"No. I came to help you find the daughter. Lady Temptress wants her with her now, as I have said. The lady wants her husband to be put into his place. And when I saw the other couple playing?" She shrugged. "I thought to have some fun while here. Men on our realm are not as you. They

95

only want to have sex when it is to procreate. I don't wish for a child ever. I enjoy fucking, not making an issue."

He didn't want to think about what would be going on in that realm if the woman called the sexual shots. Vega could see nothing getting done and people dying from not just all the sex, but simply from starving to death. And he just realized he was starving. He reached for the phone, only just realizing that they were at a hotel, not at Raw and Naked, the place he'd been when she'd shown up. A large pizza sounded so good. But he wondered if he'd be too sore to eat it.

"I'm working on two things at the moment. There is another that I've been told to find. A guy that I worked on a few years back. His parents are paying me a great deal of money to bring him to heel." She frowned, but before she could speak, he continued. "I need money now, not when this thing with your mistress is finished. I have to get a lab set up and work on some more magic. I get weaker every time I use what I have, and it's important to replenish it from time to time."

"I am instructed to give you what you need. Lady Temptress will not care if you use it to find the man too, so long as she gets what she wants. Plus, she has a need of something from you. A part of your body that you will never miss. She said she would pay you handsomely with more magic than you'd ever dream of having. Would you like it?"

He put out his hand to take it. There could never be too much magic when it came to dealing with Awnia. As he laid his hand into Rysdan's, he was disappointed to feel nothing. Not a single tremor of anything seemed to connect between them. Then when she sat back in the chair, he felt something akin to rage, an uncontrollable urge to kill Awnia.

"It is my mistress. She is going to use your body to escape from her hell that Lord Halmar put her in. You will feel pain in a moment. Then she will take you." He shook his head as the rage grew immensely until he could hardly contain it. "She hates the daughter very much. Her magic is all hate. You are feeling that as well. Soon it will even out and my mistress will enter you."

It never settled, it seemed to grow and grow. Blood seeped from his nose, and his ears rang like he was standing next to a bell and it was gonged over and over. His eyes burned, felt as if she'd put a hot poker to them, and he could no longer see out of them. As the pain consumed him, ate him alive, all he could think about besides how much he hurt was that he had to kill the daughter.

Then his body seemed to explode. Not in pain this time, but just explode. As he felt something...another person...move into his mind and rape it, Vega screamed at the images that she brought with her. Darkness was seeping into his head. The pain was no longer an issue, but something that he knew would hold him forever. Vega didn't just embrace the black hole that seemed to consume him, but fell into it with his burning eyes wide the fuck open.

He heard her then, her voice, that of Temptress. Her disappointment was profound, and she cursed him for his weakness. Vega knew that, for some reason, he was lucky for it. Otherwise his death, which was coming fast, would be longer than he wanted to have.

Then there was nothing.

CHAPTER 7

Awnia watched Margo make a cup of tea again. It was really simple, and the fact that she'd messed it up twice now made her realize how bad she was in the kitchen. But Margo had only smiled at her when she'd had to dump the cup out.

"I should have told you that you must put the tea into a ball." Awnia thought she should have known that too. Who would want to drink something that had floating things on the top? Dark weeds, they looked like to her. "And that you use only a little honey and sugar together. Not as much as you did the first time."

"I didn't know what you meant when you said that it needed to be sweeter." It had certainly been that. Painfully so. "Are you sure that you have time to show me this? I'm taking a great deal of your time from your bread. I could come back tomorrow if you want."

"I do indeed have time, and this is fun. Once I pull the bread from the oven, you and I will have a whole loaf for our lunch with a cup of the tea you'll make." As Awnia poured the boiling water into the tiny cup, all she could think about was how she'd nearly scalded them both the first time. As she finished pouring, she set the kettle—not pot, as she'd mistakenly called it—back onto the stove.

"Very good, my lady. Very good. See, I knew that you'd be a pro at this."

She'd had to learn that you didn't just put a bag into a cup and microwave some water. It was what she'd seen done nearly all her life. Now she was learning the proper way to make tea. Mrs. Payne and her son were coming for a visit, and Margo had suggested that she serve her tea. She'd had no idea it was so complicated.

When someone rang the doorbell, she didn't think anything about it. Deacon was in the front of the house polishing something or another, and she wasn't supposed to answer the door anyway. But when the doorbell pealed for the second time, she went into the small hall. Deacon was just coming down the stairs when Awnia reached beyond the door.

"Don't." Deacon stopped moving toward the door and put his hands behind his back as he stood there. "Do you know how to contact...I don't remember his name...the pride leader?"

"Samuel. Yes, we can contact him. Is his missus in trouble?" Deacon looked afraid, but she wasn't sure how to assure him, so she only shook her head. "I am to tell you not to let the person in. He and his mother Summer were nearby. He is also contacting Kennedy, his wife."

The bell rang again, and then the door rattled on the hinges. Hawk touched her mind and asked her if she was all right. She wasn't sure what to tell him either.

There is a being at the door. Not anything that I've ever encountered here. There are a few that work for Temptress. He told her not to let them in. *I'm not sure that's going to be an issue soon. They'll be able to come in if they...fuck.*

The mist came under the door and formed into its being as she told Margo and Deacon to step back. "And do not touch me. No matter what."

"Yes, my lady."

As Deacon and Margo stood near the stairs, Awnia let her magic go. It was dangerous and would give Hatter a very good idea where she was, but nothing was going to happen to these people. She felt someone, someone like Hawk, come up behind her, but he didn't speak, nor did he touch her. Awnia felt his support as if he were Hawk.

I'm Big Will. Awnia heard his voice over the roaring of her magic. *The being in front of you, I cannot touch him, but I will keep the others safe if you take care of him. All right?*

Awnia told him that she appreciated it. They both stood very still as the mist moved around the room as if he had no idea where he was going. But as soon as he stopped in front of her, she held her ground while he began to take shape.

"You are summoned," the being said in a harsh, hard voice. As soon as he was fully formed, he held out a sword. It was one that Awnia had seen before, and knew just where he'd gotten it. "Mistress Temptress of the —"

"No." He looked confused for a moment, then began again to tell her that she must come with him. "I'm not going anywhere. Especially not with you. And you'd do well to not harm those with me, or so help me, you will know pain like you've never felt before. And you'd do well to heed me. Do you know who I am?"

"Nay, and it matters little. I'm to bring you back at all costs." She smiled at him, and he took a step back. "You are to come with me gently or I will have to use force to make you come."

"So you said. But what sort of force do you have that you think will outdo mine? Would you like to see which of us is going to come out on top of this? Because if you don't think it matters who I am, then you are in for a big surprise." Letting her body heat more, she took a step toward him and touched her finger to his outstretched blade. He watched it as it melted and dripped to the floor in a puddle of steel and gold. "Are you afraid, being? Do you know what I will do to you should I touch you like this? You're flesh and blood as am I, but the difference is, I'm a good deal stronger than you."

"My lady only said that you were a prisoner and that I was to bring you back." His voice trembled a little, and she took another step toward him. "I will kill you if you continue to thrall me. It is well within my allowances from the lady that I use as much force as I deem necessary."

The woman that stepped onto the porch behind the being held a small boy in her arms as well as a gun. With a short shake of her head, Awnia had the woman lowering it, but she didn't move. Reaching out to her, hoping that the small amount of contact they'd had would be enough, Awnia warned Kennedy that there was danger.

He will kill you if he turns. Your body will not survive his touch. She nodded and moved back, then disappeared from in front of the door. *There is a back door to this house. Could you come to that and take both Margo and Deacon to safety? I fear for them. There is another being here as well. I believe him to be a friend of Hawk's. He said his name is Big Will. Please do not harm him.*

I don't want to leave you, but I'm pretty sure you have this well under control. As for Margo and Deacon, I'll try to get them to come with me, but it's doubtful that they'll leave you. Hawk has entrusted your care to them. She heard voices behind her and knew that the woman had come in. *Deacon and Big Will decided to stay, but Margo is coming with me. I could order Deacon to come, but I'd rather not. He is very loyal to you.*

Tell them not to touch me. I don't want to hurt anyone but this person in front of me. And he's going to die. Kennedy said that she would. *I'm going to kill this being. And when I do, it will be…make sure that no one touches me but Vinnie. He will be able to withstand the heat if I need help.*

You're going to be all right then? Hawk will be really pissed off if you get hurt while I'm here. Awnia told her she would. *Why do I think you're pulling me leg?*

I have no clue what that even means. But I think that Hawk would rather you all were safe than just me injured. I assure you that I do not wish to hurt either.

The being took a step toward her, and Awnia let herself go. The man in front of her screamed when she reached out and wrapped her hand around his throat. It was over in seconds. His head disintegrated in her hand even as his screams were cut off.

Turning around, she knew that she had to get out of the house. There were a great many wooden things here, and she had to be careful now. Big Will and Deacon were still standing there, and she moved by them to go out of the back of the house. Just as someone, a shifter, came out of the woods, she felt as if she might make it now. Standing in the grass, she called to Vinnie.

Come to me now, my dragon. She heard his reply, his long scream that was his animal as he shifted. There was a second coming with him. His mate, Awnia knew, and was thankful for their assistance. Turning when someone said her name, she looked at Kennedy.

"Will you cool off?" She couldn't answer her, and Kennedy seemed to have understood. "Vinnie can help you. Hawk is frantic, by the way. He can't contact you either. I've told him…I've explained to him what has happened. He's on his way with my mate and mother-in-law. They'll be here very soon."

Nodding her thanks, Awnia felt rather than heard the dragons. When they landed, their great bodies shaking the ground, she knew that she was causing more problems than these people were used to. As Vinnie took a great lung full of air into his lungs, Awnia held herself steady. When he blew his fire on her, it was going to hurt. But in the end, she'd be so much better for it.

The fire that he blew on her was welcome in its healing power. His breath was cooler than she was at the moment, and it was the only way that she'd found to keep her from getting out of control. It was the first time in centuries that she'd had to call on a dragon to do this for her. And it was only the second time that Vinnie had been the one to do it.

His mate, Abbie, took over when Vinnie had to rest. Then Awnia noticed Hawk. She had no idea how long he'd been there, she'd been so focused on cooling off. There was a man with him, but she was too hot to make out who he was. When Abbie stepped back, her heat doing what she'd needed, Awnia fell to the ground and lay there.

"She's still too hot." The voice of the man who spoke sounded familiar, but she couldn't make her mind focus right now. "Just let her be. She'll be just fine. I had no idea that a dragon could help her. First time for everything, I suppose."

Vinnie and Abbie both blew their fiery breath over her again. As she cooled off, she realized that she was naked. Looking at Hawk, who had sat in front of her, she wondered if she could make him understand what she wanted.

"They're all gone." She didn't have it in her to look around. "I've sent them away. Kennedy is in the house with Margo and Deacon. Big Will is out patrolling the grounds for me. He said that you had to kill that being. But he had no idea what it was. Samuel is also patrolling the grounds with some of Jimmy's pack, and Vinnie is in the air. He said that he knew what to look for."

"Hurt." He nodded and smiled at her. "Scared them."

"You did. Mostly Carter. But he got over it quickly when Vinnie gave him a short ride on his back. Apparently that's a cure-all for everything." He sat there for several moments before he spoke again. "I have to tell you something. Your father is here. I'm not sure how you feel about him, but he's pretty glad that you're all right. He thought you were dead all this time."

She looked up at him, then at the house. He'd been the man she didn't recognize. She knew that now. "How long?"

"He actually came to see me last night. I had to…I had no idea if it was safe or not. Or for that matter if he was your father. I called Yve." Awnia had met the faerie a long time ago. "She said not only was it your dad, but he might be a little on the pissed off side too. But not at you. He has it in his head that someone should have told him you were here. He is looking into matters now."

"Temptress?" He nodded. Awnia lay down now, her body spent but healing. She just needed a few more minutes. "That man was sent by her. Whatever she's up to, she's getting closer all the time. I know that I've said this before, but when she comes here, she'll try to kill you all."

"Yes, and we're more prepared than we were before. Your father seems to think that she's going to come here. And when she does, you'll be able to take care of her better than you think you can. And there's someone else we have to worry about. Well, actually, two more. My parents, for one, and a man by the name of Vega Pruitt. He's the man who took me to a lab when I was younger. He used his magic against me to try and appease my parents by allowing them to think that he was able to take my shifter away from me. I think you might know him as well." She shook her head, but he nodded. "I think he's your Hatter, honey, and he's working with Temptress somehow."

~~~

Hawk walked around the room. He'd already been in contact with the occupant of the room, but he felt there was more to it than that. The ghost had told him that he'd leave as soon as the owners of the house did what he wanted, like get the hell out of his house...which wasn't going to happen, because they had invested all their money into this home. And it seemed that neither party was giving an inch, as they wanted him out as well.

"You're just looking for trouble now. Why are you staying here in this room? You gonna steal something?" Hawk ignored him. "You should just go and tell them that I'm not going. I was here first. Perhaps if you tell them I'll be happy to let them...I won't bother them at all. What are you doing over there? Get on over here and talk to me. I want you to tell them they won't hear a peep out of me for the rest of their lives."

The warmth in the floor made him pause. He looked at Clar, who was standing next to the picture of the couple that had called them in. She nodded in the general direction of the ghost. It always surprised him that she could see them as well. His entire life had been so lonely with only having one other person to talk to about them. Big Will came into the room as well and braced his arms over his chest when the ghost looked like he might come at him.

They could be violent when they were angry. It didn't happen often, but enough that Hawk had begun to like having Clar with him. And Big Will was proving to be helpful as well. Clar told him through their link that she could feel something from the homeowners.

Anger. Like they're upset that they called you in. Mostly at you right now. Hawk glanced at the doorway and saw them standing there. *I think that there's more here than a ghost that won't leave.*

I feel that too. And he doesn't want me right here.

The couple moved back out of the room when he stood up and moved to the desk. As soon as they were out of sight, however, he went back to the warmth on the floor.

Working with Clar had kept him focused. Also, she made it so he didn't have to talk to people, the ones that were living, as much as he had before. Which wasn't all that much anyway. As he knelt down to the floor, the ghost started talking again. Ignoring him, he put all his energy into what was there, and then she, the warmth on the floor, made her presence known to him.

"I'm going now. Why don't you come on out with me and we'll get this done? There isn't any reason whatsoever that you have to hang around here anymore." Hawk stood up and turned to the man. "You didn't have to go and look for that. You're messing things up for me. I was gonna be able to stay here if you didn't find anything."

"But I did, didn't I? And it's not your doing but theirs, right? This isn't right. And you know it." He looked at Clar. "Call the police. There's been a murder here. The daughter of the people who own the house. They murdered her."

As she went away, he looked at the ghost. "I didn't like them at all, but they said if I kept you away from the stain, that after you left they'd call me back. I tried and tried. You'll tell them that, won't you? I don't want to leave here. I never even bothered them until they started in on the girl. It's been…they didn't deserve a girl like her. And they went and killed her."

Hawk held out the paper that was his work order. The man leaned down and read it over before looking at him again. He told him he couldn't read the paper, that he'd never gotten around to learning. "I'm terribly sorry to tell you this, but they lied to you. They said I was to evict you. Do you know what that means?"

"They aren't going to let me come back here." Hawk shook his head. "I did what they asked. My family grew up in this house. There are memories here that I love. I miss them so much. I just wanted to stay here and then they hurt her. I tried to…she is terrified, that girl. I think…why? Why would someone do such a thing?"

Hawk never asked the people he worked with to cross over, wherever that might be. But he did listen to the people that he found. Like his book and his knife, they were once things that had a purpose, and he hated to hurt them.

"You won't have to deal with them anymore. I think that once the police get here, they're going to take them away for a long time." Hawk heard the sirens going off even as he turned to the stain again. "Can you tell me what happened here? She's so confused that all she can do is whimper, and I can't really talk to her yet."

"She came home late from some dance or something. They were both waiting for her. To be honest, I went with her, to kind of keep an eye on her, but she was a good girl. Never lied to them about where she'd been or what she'd been doing. Her and that friend of hers just hung out, but never drank nothing like they said she did." Hawk asked him how they'd figured out about him. "That girl told them. She said that I was here. I don't know why she told them, but she let them know she could talk to me and I talked back. She's smart. I enjoyed her company. I let them know right away that I knew what they'd done to her. But when they started making noises about calling you in, I got scared. I don't want to leave. But she's not liking it here much. We're going to keep each other company until she thinks on what she wants to do."

"They murdered her and buried her in the back." The ghost had no answer, but when Hawk turned to him he could see him looking in the corner. The girl was there, but she was too new for him to see. Anyone who had been dead less than five years had difficulty staying in a state where he could see them. "Tell her that I'm taking care of this."

"She said to tell you thanks. And that her diary is up in her room. Under some floor boards. She said for you not to read it, she'd be too embarrassed, but to tell the police." Hawk said he would. "She said...I'm thinking that she wants to go on over to the other place about now. I might just go with her. You never preached to me like that other man did. He was here for ten minutes and I sent him on his way."

Hawk had a feeling he knew who it was but said nothing. There were all kinds of people out there taking advantage of people in need. Not the living, for as much as he needed them, he didn't care for them all that much. As the police came into the room, he told them what he'd found. Two of the officers were men he knew, one of whom he'd had some dealings with, and not all of them good. When he spoke, Hawk simply walked away.

"I asked you a question."

Before he could say anything more, he heard Big Will speaking. He had no idea what he might have said to the officer, but Hawk was able to leave the room without incident.

He wanted to go home. Awnia was there with her father, and he needed to be with her. He'd not wanted to leave the house at all, but Clar had called him this morning, frantic, and he'd come here to assist. The ghost had been giving her a hard time and she wasn't going to leave without answers. She looked up at him as they left the house over an hour later. Big Will had said he was going to work on something else.

"The father is being taken in. His wife is claiming that she had no idea what he'd done to their daughter." Hawk nodded. He'd heard from the ghost that they had both been in on it. "She's claiming that someone else murdered their daughter by coming in while they were gone. The mother has no reason for why they buried her in the back. They're trying to claim that her daughter was a run away and had left before. I don't think that's what the cops are finding out in the diary. How did you know about the book, anyway?"

"Your ghost told me." She nodded and told him that it figured. "You're doing well, Clar. It's just going to take you some time for your name to get around to other ghosts."

"That's probably the strangest thing anyone ever said to me." He laughed with her. "I'm going over to your house. Summer invited all us women to the house to get to know Awnia. I like her, by the way."

"Me too." Hawk told her that Awnia's father was there. "He said he's going to protect her. And talk to her about us being mates. She still believes we're not. I think there's something that neither of them are telling me, but I don't know what it is as yet."

"I think you might be right. I think Vinnie might know something as well, but he said she'd asked him not to say anything. I think he wants to, but he is very loyal to her." He nodded as they got into the car. Hawk reached his hand into his pocket to stroke the medallion that Samuel had given him to find Awnia with. It warmed under his touch, as it did every time he touched it.

"Did you know that there are all kinds of ghosts out there?" He had no idea why he was telling Clar this, but now that he'd started, he figured it couldn't hurt. "There are so many different types. Some that just go about their existence without ever bothering anyone. Then there are the mean types. The ones that break things, move other stuff around to be pissy. And then there are the ones that have no idea that they're dead, and wander around trying to figure out why everyone is ignoring them. And believe it or not, they're the ones that are the hardest to work with."

She looked at him as if she didn't believe him, but he assured her that he was telling her no lie. "The only ones I've dealt with are like the guy in there. Just wanting to be left alone for one reason or another. How do you deal with the ones that aren't aware?"

"About six years ago I was looking at a few pieces that were bought from an estate auction. There were several pieces, most of them crap, but there were two that caught my eye. The large desk that had been unearthed in a warehouse, and a large fainting couch." He thought about the desk. "I asked to purchase it and was told that I could have it. There were things about it that I knew needed to be repaired, but they were minor compared to what I knew was in it."

"What?" He grinned at her when she told him to hurry up and tell her. "You tell the worst kinds of stories. I mean they're good, don't get me wrong, but you make me want to pound on your head the way you make it suspenseful. Samuel does that too. I'm pretty sure he's learned it from you."

"I have been tutoring him on the art of pissing you off. I think he's doing very well. Even Kennedy cursed me in Gallic the other night. At least I think it was cursing. Anyway, the desk belonged to a very famous mobster, and he'd used the desk for all sorts of deals." She glanced at him as she stopped at a light. "The desk knew everything that man had done. Things no one else knew."

"You're shitting me." He laughed and told her he was not. "Is there hidden treasure? Maybe a bank job that has never been recovered? That would be fun, to be the one to find it after all these years. It has been years, right?"

"Yes, since the thirties." Hawk closed his eyes as he continued. "There was treasure that only he and I could appreciate. Stories that he told me that were humorous and quite unbelievable at times. But they were good ones. I'm thinking of using the desk and writing his stories. Not for the money or fame, if there would be any, but for the pure enjoyment of having them written down for others to enjoy."

It had only been a half-baked plan until recently. He'd actually thought about it again when a private investigation firm had contacted him a few months ago about his family and the fact that he'd been declared dead.

Apparently his grandmother on his mother's side had left him a great deal of money, as well as the house that his parents had been living in. And just last week, after he'd found that they'd hired Vega again to find him and bring him to them, he'd made arrangements to have them removed from his house and his life. Forever. The lawyer was all for the idea, in fact had asked if he could do it immediately. Hawk had told him to go for it.

But the story idea had surfaced again then, and he wanted to do it. He'd even talked it over with Awnia when she'd seen the desk in his building. But now that he'd told someone else, he thought harder about it.

"I think that's a wonderful—"

He opened his eyes when she didn't finish. The street in front of them, his street, was lined with cruisers and fire trucks. All he could think about was Awnia and that she'd gotten too hot. As soon as the car slowed, he was out and shifting even as he grabbed up the medallion and held it in his hand as he went. Hawk was in the air before Clar even got out of the car.

Samuel was talking to Awnia when he landed near them. At his nod, Awnia turned to him, and he felt relief. He had no idea what had happened and really didn't care so long as she was all right. As she made her way to him, he took off to the sky again, watching that she could follow him.

It wasn't me. He heard her as he led her deeper into the woods. *I mean, it was sort of me, but I didn't burn anything up. The building was a hazard anyway.*

Which building? And so you know, as soon as I get you out here far enough, I'm going to fuck you. She paused, then moved forward again. *What happened?*

I went out to the barn, the one on the back of the property. Deacon said it might be a good place to hide if someone came for me. You know, a place that I could cool off. But all I did was turn on the light and walked around. It was perfect by the way, steel roof, but the electrical was messy. She moved a few more steps in. *Are you really going to fuck me?*

He landed in front of her and shifted. As soon as he did, Hawk pulled her into his arms and kissed her, putting as much of his need into it as he could. Tearing at both of their clothing, he held her to his cock, rocking into her even as her clothing started to fall to the ground. When her breasts were naked, he took the right one into his mouth and suckled it hard. Hawk moaned out her name when she wrapped her hand around his cock.

"I want to taste you." He nodded and turned so that his back was against the closest tree. But instead of tasting him, she took another step back and stared at him. His cock ached now to be inside of her, either her pussy or her mouth. At this point he didn't care. "I've never had a man come down my throat before. Will you? Come down my throat, I mean?"

"Yes. Gladly." She nodded and bent at the waist. Her tongue on his cock nearly had him come all over her. "I'd like for you to turn around and show me that pretty ass like that first." Awnia turned for him and bent again. Christ, she looked delicious.

"Like this?" He nodded and moved up behind her. She was just too irresistible to leave alone. "I can't suck your cock if you're going to fuck me. And I want to suck you, Hawk. I think I need it more than I need to breathe."

Fisting his cock, Hawk slid it over her juices that flowed from her to her creamy thighs. Even as she moved back against him, he moved in and out of her with his crown. Using his free hand, Hawk moved to her pussy and soaked his fingers with her cream, then moved it along the tight pucker of her ass. He'd never wanted to fuck a woman there, but her he did.

"To think that this little hole is all mine too." He moved his finger into her as he slid deeper into her with his cock. "You're so hot. I wonder why you never scorch me when I'm inside of you."

She stood and turned then. His cock was wet with her juices as he stepped back from her. He could see by the look in her face that she was afraid, and he nearly told her he was kidding, but she took another step back and spoke. Her face told him that she was upset, and he tried to think what he'd done or said to do it.

"Did he give it to you? Vinnie did, didn't he?" He knew what she was talking about the moment she asked. "Where is it?"

Hawk held out his hand and showed her the medallion. He was almost afraid she was going to ask for it back, but she shied away from it. He closed his fingers around it as she started pacing. He was afraid now. Unsure what it meant for him to have it, and more afraid that she was going to tell him he had no right to still have it. More so than he'd been when he'd thought that she'd been hurt earlier.

"It's a part of me. That thing you hold is a small part of me. I gave it to Vinnie a long...a very long time ago, when he thought he was my mate. It didn't work." He looked at it again. This time he really looked at it by raising it to the sun and looking directly through the stone.

"It moves." She nodded but said nothing else. "What happened to Vinnie? I'm assuming that something he was supposed to do with this didn't work, and it hurt him somehow. That's the reason you're so afraid for me to see if I'm your mate, isn't it? You don't want me hurt."

"The witch told me how it would work by telling me this poem. 'The wearer is true. The mate is forever. The heart knows what no one else can know.' I thought that I was in love with Vinnie and him me. I know that he loves me, but not...." She turned to him. "We thought he was supposed to wear it. I have no idea why we thought something so mundane would work, but as soon as he put it around his neck, it began to burn into his body. Not just his body, but his heart. It was trying to burn out his heart. I think because it wasn't true to mine. Not that he didn't love me, but that he didn't love me in the right way."

"It won't burn me, Awnia. I'm your mate." She shook her head, and he nodded. "I am. You have to believe me. If I have to prove it to you, I will, but I love you, truly and forever."

"I won't have you die to find out. You will, too, if you try to claim me with that. You'll die and I'll be alone." He reached for her again, this time not thinking about her naked body next to his, but the simple and profound need to just hold her. "I love you. I can't believe how much I do, but I love you."

"And I love you. We'll figure this out. I promise."

CHAPTER 8

Frederick looked over at his wife, Bambi, as they were going down the highway. She'd been on that blasted phone since they'd left or, to be truthful, since they'd been evicted. He needed some answers from her, and was tempted to just knock the phone out of her hand to get her attention. Finally, she put it down.

"That was Mr. Pruitt. That dreadful man said that he will be giving us his bill soon. He no longer needs our business. To think how much we've paid him already. Well, we will not pay it. He was to complete the job and he has not." Frederick looked away from her. This was her fault anyway, the doctors had said so. "Are you listening to me?"

"Yes, you're bitching about money again. It matters little if he sends us a bill or not, we've not the funds to pay him." Frederick glared at her. "Your mother really fucked us over this time. I thought you said it would all work out. So far as I can see, nothing at the moment is working out. Except for that thing of yours." He still to this day would not acknowledge he had a son. Especially not the one he'd been given at the hospital. He, that thing, belonged solely to her.

Frederick had been informed...that was what the little insurance lawyer had said. "You're informed that there will be no more funds coming from the estate as of ten days ago." So far as he knew there was plenty of money for them, and said as much to him. The man, Howard something, had handed him a thick envelope and smiled. He should have known with a smile like that he'd be up to no good. This had been just yesterday morning, and then that eviction bitch had shown up today. But in hindsight he knew that he should have made arrangements for things to be put aside the moment the lawyer had left them.

"You have a son by the name of Russel Hawkmen?" Frederick remembered looking around to see if anyone had heard Howard say his name aloud. "We had a firm look into some reports that we had about him. And you and your wife. You lied to us, Mr. Hawkmen. He is not dead as you have claimed. And that, sir, is insurance fraud."

Frederick had known that was going to come back and bite them in the ass. He'd told Bambi when they'd hatched this plan that there were just too many things that could go wrong. And the fact that they knew where he was and what he was up to notwithstanding, it was still a lie that was going to bring them down. The thing was alive and well.

"Mr. Russel Hawkmen called our office two days ago, and we are making sure that he is aware of the estate and its contents that his grandmother left him when she passed nine years ago. He is not happy to know that he was declared dead by you. A paper filed with your name on it is now in the hands of the law firm that is looking into other allegations. You and your wife have been living off his kind generosity for all this time, and he has said that he'd like you to stop." He asked him why, what business it was of anyone's what he and his wife had done? "I'm pretty sure, sir, as you should know, that lying about inheritance is a crime. And as it is his money and his property that you are living in, he can pretty much tell you whatever he wants. And what he wants is you two gone. As of right now."

As soon as the lawyer had been seated in the living room with strict orders to the staff not to let him out of their sight, Frederick had gone to find Bambi. She, of course, wasn't home, and he'd had to resort to asking the staff where she was. The maid that he'd caught eating a big breakfast in the kitchen had no idea where she was. Nor for that matter, how to contact her. He'd had to wait for the cook so he could ask her.

The new cook and butler were nothing like the last staff had been. They had, at least, had meals done on time. This crew was mouthy and lazy. He hated the way his food always tasted like they'd microwaved it rather than cooked it.

Frowning as the car carried them further down the highway, Frederick realized how off track he'd gotten while thinking about the attorney and the eviction woman, and where she'd gotten off kicking him out of his house.

"Where is my wife?" Frederick had asked the cook, who looked at him, then at the man standing next to her. "My wife. The woman who hired you. Where is she?"

"I believe that Mrs. Hawkmen has gone to the hairdresser, sir." The butler had the nerve to look down his nose at him. "Sir, there is a matter of our wages. Our checks have bounced and the bank is saying that you no longer have access to the account, so our checks are void. Also, we have just been informed by mail that you are no longer our employer. I do believe we have a contract. We will be expecting you to honor your agreement with us."

Frederick had left them standing there. His wife was missing, and that jack wipe had had the nerve to talk to him about his contract? It had taken Frederick nearly three hours to chase her down. When she came in the door to the house, she'd been pissed. Her credit cards, she'd told him, had been canceled. He was glad that he'd finally told the lawyer that he'd have to make an appointment to see him, and shown him to the door before she'd gotten home.

"And that stupid bitch at the store took them from me and cut them up right there where everyone could see her. The nerve of them. I'm going to sue." He told her that the woman had every right to do it, according to the lawyer. "What lawyer? Ours would never do such a thing, and if it is someone in their firm, I want them fired."

So Frederick had spent the next two hours explaining to her what had happened and why. Now here they were on the road. He had no idea how they'd even gotten this car, much less how they were ever going to live this crap down once it was fixed. If it ever got fixed. He looked over at Bambi when his thoughts were making him somewhat ill.

"What do we hope to accomplish by going to see him?" Frederick had no idea when they left where they were even going, and now he thought this was as harebrained as anything that she'd come up with so far. "I mean, I doubt very much he's going to welcome us with open arms. Not that I'd let that thing touch me."

"And why not? We're his parents, and I'm pretty sure that trumps him being upset with us. Besides, we've called off Mr. Pruitt, haven't we? And it's not like he could live there now anyway. I mean, they put locks on all the doors." He wanted to point out that Mr. Pruitt had called himself off, and that the locks were there because he and she had been physically removed as of that morning, but she hated it when he pointed out the flaws in her logic. This car they were using was a rental, which they'd promised the driver their son would pay for, and it wasn't even a good one at that. "Besides, like I said, we're his parents, no matter how badly he's messed up our lives. He'll have to fix this for us. He owes us for bringing him up."

Again there was a flaw in her thinking, but he had learned long ago not to argue points with her. Not when she was so sure she was right. Instead, Frederick looked out the window and thought about what they'd had to leave behind.

Money was not all of it, but a great deal. He'd grown quite accustomed to being wealthy and all the comforts it afforded him. Trips to wherever he wanted to go, and whatever he'd wanted to buy once he got there. Clothing from the best places that were fitted to him, not from a rack, was a luxury that he was very upset to let go. There was the fact that he'd never lifted a finger to do a thing around the house either. Not that he noticed when someone cleaned up after him, but he didn't have to do it, so that was perfect. He'd had not just a closet of clothing, but a wall devoted to shoes. Another to watches, something he'd learned to appreciate more than he had the money. Well, not quite true. The money had afforded him the ability to buy them, but he loved having all the jewels.

Late in his life, he'd discovered his love for watches. Old, new, he didn't care, so long as it was expensive and looked good on him. He supposed having several hundred of them just lying in boxes in drawers was sort of stupid and a waste of money, but he'd had it to spend and he liked them. Now those, too, were being inventoried by some person that wouldn't know their value. Touching what was his, what he'd worked hard to acquire, and things that he had loved even more than his wife.

"He'll take us back into his lives once I have a word or two with him. Then we'll get this silly thing taken care of with the money, and it'll be just like we never left." Frederick didn't think it would be that easy. And to be frank about it, he really wasn't pleased that they'd have to beg their...he hated to use the word...but have to beg their son to reconsider what he was doing to them. The fucking little prick should be happy they didn't hire a man to kill him again. A blot like him should have been drowned at birth, not allowed to live among decent people.

"I think we should just have him killed." There, he'd said it again. When Bambi didn't say anything, he looked at her. "I told you just after we were given the news that you'd had a defective child that we should have taken him on that trip with us. A small boy falling off the side of the boat wouldn't have been that hard to believe. And we'd be living off him, not the other way around."

"Well, it's a moot point now. We don't have the money to pay anyone, and the boat, like the plane, is now off limits to us." He nodded. His boat had been taken too. His lovely Desire in the Sand. "But as soon as we sit him down and talk this over, we'll have it all back."

She kept saying that. He wasn't sure if she was saying it to convince herself or him, but he really didn't care so long as they were back in their home. Frederick was, if this worked out the way Bambi was saying, going to hire someone to kill that thing and Bambi, and be done with the whole mess of them. Because, as much as he loved the money, her money, he disliked Bambi.

Mostly, she was stupid, and when she wasn't saying something profoundly dumb—like every time she opened her mouth—she was dressing in a style...Frederick looked over at her...or whatever it was that she wore, that made him ill. She was entirely too old to be wearing a blue and white striped sailor suit with white boots. And today's outfit was only marginally ridiculous compared to the bright yellow dress—the very short micro-dress, she'd called it—which was her costume when she'd first gotten up. It hurt his eyes every time he'd looked at it.

When the police and another little lawyer had shown up this morning, he'd been in his bathrobe and slippers. He was just having his first cup of coffee poured for him, and his warm croissant was sitting on the china he loved with butter slowly melting over it. The butler, whatever the hell his name was, had come in while he'd been enjoying his quiet time—before Bambi got up—to inform him he had a visitor.

"Tell them to make an appointment." The man only stood there. Ever since yesterday, the man had been snotty to him, even going so far as to get lippy with him. "Well? Tell them to go away. I'm busy."

"I'm afraid that won't work, Mr. Hawkmen." The girl had breezed into his dining room like she owned it. Then she slapped a blue paper in front of him, spilling his coffee over his napkin. He looked at the man... damn it all to hell, what was his name? Butler was all he could think of. Anyway, he'd stood there as if he was waiting to find out what she was doing there as well. And he'd had to dismiss him three times before he left the room.

"What is the meaning of this? I'm going to call my lawyer." She moved out of the way, and there he stood in the doorway, holding his briefcase in one hand and his hat in the other. Albert Daniels had looked decidedly nervous.

"What the hell is going on here, Albert? I thought you told this woman to leave us alone."

"The insurance company has located your son, Frederick. You and the missus are in big trouble, I'm afraid. I was informed yesterday that you were told this. And me too, as a matter of record. I might lose my practice and license over this. Did you know he was alive?" He nodded slowly, trying to think what the hell he was supposed to do now. "They're well within their rights to do this, sir. Mr. Hawkmen, your son has all the papers—"

"Never call him my son." He'd stood up then, spilling coffee all over the papers and more on his robe. The little spit of a woman had laughed then, and he'd actually drawn back to hit her.

"Do it. Please do it. Because whatever hole your son puts you in, I'll own that too." He'd put his hand down, but it had burned to hit her. "Mr. Hawkmen, it gives me great pleasure to tell you that you are being evicted. As of right now. This gentleman here will escort you to the bedroom to dress. You will only take what you need to cover yourself for the day. No jewelry, no money, and certainly no luggage. Your wife will be watched as well. So if I were you, I'd try really hard not to steal the silverware."

"I have to have some money to live on until you're fired." She'd only laughed at him. "You can't possibly think that I'm leaving this house with nothing. This is my home. My things are here."

"Not any more, they're not. They belong, as does everything else you have been using here, to your son." He growled at her, and he knew she'd called the thing his son on purpose.

Frederick turned to Bambi when she shook him, bringing him out of his musing. He was glad for it, he supposed, but he still disliked this entire mess.

"Are you even listening to a word I'm saying?" He had to admit to her that he'd not been. "Why do I even bother when you're not even...? I was asking you if you could hug that person. It might go a long way to getting on his good side."

"Touch him?" He had to suppress the urge to gag. "I will no more touch him than I would a dead animal on the road. It's bad enough that I have to go and beg to him like a pauper, but I will not touch him. And if you suggest that again, I shall have you leave me along the side of the road and have you come back for me."

"I didn't think so. We'll have to think of something else." He shivered again as he thought of touching that thing.

"How do you even live with yourself knowing that he came from your body? Or worse yet, that he nursed from you?" Frederick looked at her breasts. "I've not even had the desire to look at them since we found out what he was. I'd have had them removed. Both of them."

"It's a burden." Bambi leaned back in the seat. "That hospital covered their tracks well. I've been all over those books of theirs to try and figure out whose thing they gave us. Our child is out there, and he might need us. If we could prove it, prove that he's not ours, we'd be able to have all our pretty things back. But according to their records, that thing was the only one born that day. Fat chance. I saw all those other brats that day. Remember that woman down the hall from me? Forever having the father of her brat come in to see her and bring her flowers. I'm glad you never did that."

Again Frederick didn't point out that they'd had numerous blood tests done, and each of them had proven that the thing was theirs. He glanced at his wife of forty years. How could she have done this to them...to him? To bring such a monster into their lives? As for bringing her flowers in the hospital? He'd made sure that she was well cared for, hadn't he? And so far as he'd been concerned, the hospital was for her enjoyment. He'd never intrude on that.

"He's going to have to die." Frederick looked at Bambi when she spoke softly. "That thing, it's going to have to die. If we don't take care of it, it'll come back to haunt us for years, and we just can't have that. What if it...oh Frederick, what if it breeds?"

"Christ." He'd never even considered that. To have more of them in their family? It would be...it would be like having a family of monsters living with them. "You make the arrangements. I'll figure out how we can pay for this."

"He'll pay for it. For his own death, he'll pay." She leaned her head back and smiled. "We should have done this years ago. When he was a child. Like I told you on the boat. No one would have missed him."

Frederick had an overwhelming urge to hit her. That had been his idea. He'd just...damn it all to hell, he was getting sick of playing second fiddle to her insanity. He supposed that she really wasn't insane so much as she was a backstabbing bitch. Smiling, he thought that suited her and added it to his mental list of names to call her when he was alone. And he was putting her name higher on the list of people he was going to take care of as soon as he was flush again.

Frederick leaned back in his seat as well. They had a long way to go to see that monster of theirs. He had no idea where they were going to stay when they got there. He was hungry and they didn't have a penny between them. He'd barely been able to scrape up enough money to get them each a cup of the most horrid coffee they could afford. But she was right about this. If they could get him to take them back, even for a little while, they could horde some money, have him killed, then live like they'd grown accustomed to all these years. Then for the insurance, he'd have her killed as well.

"First things first," he whispered to himself. "Make the thing believe we're changed. That we want him in our lives."

Yes, he thought, that was a good plan.

~~~

"I'm sure that they're on their way." Hawk nodded to his "lawyer." Thor had told him that she could pull this eviction off, and apparently she had. His parents were no longer in his home, and as of right now, things that had belonged to them were being packed up and taken to a local charity. "That mother of yours? She's something else. What the hell is wrong with her? And good Christ, Hawk, who the fuck buys her clothes? A blind kid? I mean really, her closet, when I got a chance to see inside of it, resembled a box of brightly colored crayons that had been melted down and splattered on everything."

"Yeah. When I was younger, before they found out that I was different, I used to not look at her directly. Once she had on a green and purple pinstriped blouse with a large dotted skirt. Mother thought she was the height of fashion. As for me? She seems to think that having me as a son is some sort of black mark against her. And me being a monster—her words, not mine—is something that should and will be stricken from her life." Thor grinned, and he had a feeling she was thinking of something diabolical. "What is going on in that mind of yours?"

"Nothing. Well, plenty, but not much I'd share with you. What are your plans for the house? Because, I have to tell you, that sucker is decked out in the most rich and famous things. I used the toilet and there was so much gold in it that I had to put on my shades. And shit, did you know that a whole wall in that room is a fucking fountain that is full of fish? Does she fucking fish while she's shitting? Pick out the one for her dinner while she's wiping her hoo-ha?"

"You know, you have the most delicate way of putting things. And I have no idea what that room looks like. Or any other room in that house, other than the few rooms I was in. And by now, I'm sure that they've been sandblasted and redone several times." He handed her a thick envelope. "What can you tell me about these?"

She thumbed through the pictures that had come to him that morning. They were mostly blurred, taken from a phone some years ago, before the technology really caught up with the times. Hawk knew when she came across the ones of Awnia.

"When?" He told her five months ago. "This guy, is he the one that you were telling me about? This…Pruitt person?"

"Yes. I think that my tormentor and hers are the same person. She refers to him as Hatter." The doorway was darkened and they both looked up. Awnia stood there as if she wasn't sure she'd be welcomed. Before he could say for her to come in, Thor stood up.

"I've not had the pleasure yet. I'm Tania, but the only person who calls me that is Kaleb, and only during sex. Call me Thor." Awnia blushed deeply but came into the room.

"If you need to not touch me, tell me now. I tend to feel people up so I can have a connection."

"I'm sorry, but if you touch me without permission, it'll end badly for you. I'm a sun goddess, and even if the name didn't imply it, I'm sort of hot." Thor nodded and put out her hand. "I'll have a connection to you as well. I mean, more than likely stronger than yours to me."

"I'm good with that." The two of them touched, and he could see the moment that Thor realized she might have bitten off more than she could chew. When she pulled back and sat there for several minutes, Hawk laughed.

"You're speechless." She grinned at him. "I think I'll have to write this down, Thor is speechless about something. I'd alert the media, but I think that they'd need a few days to confirm it. You are never without a nasty comment or something snarky to say."

"Fuck off." Thor looked at Awnia as she continued. "He hurt you. That guy, Hatter, he hurt you more than you've ever told anyone. I'd say you got in a few good punches too, but what I don't understand is why you didn't just kill him right off?"

"I couldn't. I was taught that to kill, to cause harm, would come back on me. I knew that what he was doing was diabolical, but he was also, at one time, a human. And to our kind, they are to be treated with some sort of respect." Thor snorted. "I agree. You need to earn it before you get it. I'm leaning in that direction the next time I see him. And he'll continue until he's dead or I am." Awnia looked at Hawk, but he knew she was speaking to both of them. "I've heard from Yve. She said that my mother has escaped from her cell in a way that has made it difficult for the guard to find her. I'm thinking she's moved into something, like another object, to escape and is here now. It is said that she has a servant that answers only to her…Rysdan. She would have assisted her."

When Halmar entered the room, both Thor and he stood up. The man had never made them do this, it was just that his stance, his whole persona, made you want to bow before him. He frowned at them as he kissed Awnia on the forehead.

"I've just left home." He sat down on the couch and looked at them. "Would you mind terribly if I stayed here for a while? Just until this thing with Temptress is finished. She can be something of a cunt, and if I'm here, I might be able to help you with her. If nothing else, I might be able to assist in telling you her faults. She has a great many of those."

"I don't care, but you'll have to clear it with Awnia. It's her house too." Hawk waited for her to say that it wasn't her home but his, but she only nodded. Last night had proven a great deal of fun, having her bend to his will. "When we have things in the proper order here, I'd like to have a word or two with you, sir. It's about this magic that I seemed to have inherited. This morning I nearly severed my arm when I reached for a screwdriver."

"Sure, sure. You'll get more and more of it as time goes on. I think it has to do with the way you and Awnia touch all the time." There was a bit of anger there, but not much. Hawk wanted to tell him they did more than touch, but was reasonably sure he knew. Halmar looked around the room before continuing. "I might be persuaded to make some improvements too. I noticed that the faeries are moving things about, changing things to suit the room and the people in it. They do that with me as well. Not allowed in the bedroom, however, I noticed. That proved a little dangerous at my home when I kept stubbing my blasted toe

130

on a chair. It would be in one place when I went to the bathroom, and a different place when I returned. Do you put down rules as well? To keep guests safe?"

"The bedrooms are off limits so long as they are occupied. If you'd like for them to play in your room while here, you'll have to tell them. Or tell Margo. She's in charge of them, so to speak." Halmar nodded, and he looked at Thor, who was still looking over the pictures.

"This one here, who is this?" She handed it to him, then to Awnia. Leaving the couch, Halmar pulled a chair over and looked as well. "I swear I've seen him before. It'll come to me."

The man she'd pointed to was standing with a group of other men. His father was there, as well as his mother, but they were both facing the camera, while this man wasn't. He was looking back at the building that was behind them all. Hawk had no clue who he was.

"I know him." Halmar smiled. "His name eludes me at the moment, but he's a god. A little higher in the work detail than I am, but we did know each other for a time. I think he might be friends still with that faerie of Vinnie's.... Yve might know him. Good guy. Works hard, as I remember. There are a lot of us gods here on this earth that have day jobs. It's sort of boring having it all, all the time."

"Good guy or not, what is he staring so intently at that building for? And he doesn't look happy about it." Halmar said he didn't know, but when he looked at Awnia, he had a feeling she knew. "Honey? What is that building?"

"They call it the slaughter house." She shivered as she continued. "That's where they took me the first time that he caught me. There were others there; most of them had been encased in magic to hold them. I never knew what it was called until later. It's where we're brought to try and kill us.

Our magic will then go to the one who managed to murder us."

"A house of black magic?" She nodded at her father, who had stood up. "Where is this place, do you know? I'd very much like to take care of this building right now. And if that god has anything to do with it, I can assure you, he'll be dealt with as well."

"As of the moment he took action on this will of his grandmother's, Hawk owns it." Thor pulled a small tablet from her bag on the floor. "It was never one of the places that were mentioned in your grandmother's will, so I can only assume your parents bought it later. That, and about ten other buildings that were until recently being renovated. But into what, I've never been able to figure out. You told me to get rid of anything your parents might have had, and that's what I'm having done. Today it was on my list of things to ask you about. I'm not sure what they were used for or being fitted to use for, but it's going to be up to you to decide."

"Destroy them." Thor nodded. "Any of them that have had any connection to this kind of work, I want it gone. Make sure that if there is any of that kind of work going on at the other buildings, those people see the error of their ways as well. If Halmar wants to go with you, let him."

"Will do." She handed him three more pictures, two of which he had no idea about and one he could only stare at. "Your parents, right?"

"Yes. These I have no idea. Do you?" She shook her head as he laid them back down on the desk before speaking. "How long before they arrive? I'd very much like to have as many shifters and other beings here as possible. It's time to show my parents what the true meaning of family is."

Thor stood up as she spoke. "They'll arrive in about two days. There is a little problem with the car they've rented. The guy driving is a buddy of mine, and told me he has some nice verbal exchanges coming from them. He said that it's part of his job to make sure that they're aware of the recording going on before they leave with him. Marco said that they've either forgotten about it or simply don't care who knows how they feel. They don't care much for you, do they?"

"No. I've been referred to as the 'monster' for most of my life." Thor nodded and told him she was sorry. "Not your problem, but I'm sick of what they're doing. I'd very much like to take care of this once and for all. Thanks for your help on it. I can't tell you how much I'm glad this is getting finished."

"Consider it done. When they arrive...I'll talk to Kennedy and Summer. If anyone can organize this army, they can." Hawk nodded at Thor. "Have the two of you thought about what's going to happen when they get here? I mean, what's really going to happen? They're going to do some major sucking up. Can you turn them down? Once and for all?"

"Yes."

Thor stared at him for a long few minutes. He didn't flinch from her intense stare. If anyone could see his resolve, it would be her. When she nodded and told him she had faith in him, Hawk thought it was the best compliment anyone had ever given him.

When she left, so did Halmar, saying something about getting his suite set up. Hawk had a moment to wonder where he was sleeping if he thought there was a suite, but Awnia spoke first.

"I want you."

CHAPTER 9

"Come here." Awnia shook her head and stood up. "Then how am I to take you if you don't come to me?"

"I said I wanted you, so I'll take you." She noticed that his eyes darkened with desire, and she moved to the door. "I don't want anyone to disturb us. I've asked Deacon to make sure that no one comes to find us. He said it would be his pleasure."

She locked the door, then stood there while she unbuttoned her shirt. She was glad now that she'd taken the time with her dressing this morning, and was doubly glad that Kennedy had taken her shopping. When she pulled the shirt off, she could see that Hawk appreciated it as well.

"I got some new things yesterday." He nodded and rolled his chair back from his desk. "I love the feeling of silk against my skin. And it makes my nipples feel very hard."

"Come here, Awnia. I need to taste how hard they are." She stood there until he stood up. "I'm not going to wait much longer. The thought of having you naked is making my cock very hard."

"Show me." He opened his button and then lowered the zipper. As soon as he reached his hand into his pants and stroked himself, she moaned. "Show me, Hawk. I want to see your luscious cock."

He freed himself and then pulled his pants down, freeing his cock for her. When he stood up after removing them from his legs, his shirt covered him from her view. He continued to rub his hand over his cock, and she watched as a stain appeared on the tail of his shirt.

"You have to show me what you have beneath your pants before I go any further. Like, do your panties match your bra? Are they as skimpy and silky? Are they wet with your warm juices?"

"I'm very wet for you." She pulled her pants off by bending over completely. She knew that he could see her breasts...it was why she'd bent this way. Standing up, she stood before him now in just the little set that she'd paid a fortune for.

"What are your plans for taking me? I have a few ideas on how I'd like to be taken, if you don't mind." She shook her head, not sure she could speak as he cupped his balls and moaned. "I'd very much like to fuck you while you bend over that chair. Then when I'm finished with that, I'd like to suck that pretty pussy of yours until you fill me up. And, baby, I'm starved for you."

"I'd like that. But I want to suck your cock." He pulled his shirt off his body and dropped it to the floor. He was hard, his cock thick with need, and she wanted to lick the cum that dripped in a long stream from him. She moved forward, thinking of all the things she wanted to do to him.

Going to her knees in front of him, she took the pearly cum into her mouth. Licking him clean, she moaned when he pulled her to him. His cock filled her mouth and throat, and he cried out as he held her still.

"You do that again and I'm going to come right now. I've been wanting to do this to you for hours...days, I think."

Awnia moved her tongue around the crown of his cock when he pulled back. His taste exploded in her mouth, and she held his hips so that she could take her time with him without him rushing her.

"I'm going to come, love." His voice was harsh, and his fingers curled into her hair as he started fucking her mouth harder. Each time he slid past her throat, she knew that he was going to fill her. "Christ."

This taste of him was much stronger; his cum was hot, salty, and there was so much of him as he came. He pounded her mouth, holding her head with both his hands, and all she could think about was her pussy and how much she wanted him to take her that way. When Hawk jerked from her and pulled her from the floor, she stumbled as he nearly tossed her to the chair. She was so needy that she staggered twice more before she was close enough to it to hold on.

"Bend over and hang on." She had just grabbed the arms when he slammed into her from behind. Crying out her release only seemed to fuel him as he grabbed a handful of her hair again and held her up while he fucked her. "Come. Now."

His fingers didn't just slide into her pussy, but seemed to dig into her. Her clit, swollen from need, was so sensitive that she cried out again when he pinched her. Her climax took her breath away even as he continued to pound her to another peak. As soon as she felt his teeth scrape along her shoulder, she tilted her neck and gave him her throat. His teeth tore into her pulse and brought her again. His roar against her throat had her grabbing his hand and helping him while she came again. This time, he came with her.

Hawk held her as he fed from her. She'd not realized until that moment that he'd needed it. As he sealed the wound at her throat, she closed her eyes while he wrapped his arms around her and turned her to his chest. His cock was still thick. She could feel him harden again the longer they stood there. As his hands moved up and down her spine, Awnia felt as if she could stay there with him like that forever.

"Do you have any idea how much I'd like to take you to our bed and make slow and easy love to you?" Moaning, she snuggled under his chin and kissed his slowing pulse. "Will you bite me? Feed from me again?"

"Would you like that?" For an answer, he shifted her around and held her mouth to his throat. Awnia took a deep breath of him. His scent was so warm and earthy that she felt dizzy with desire again. "I've never bitten anyone but you before. Did you like it?"

"Oh yes, baby. Very much so. Lick where you wish to bite me. The feeling I get when you sink your teeth into me, the thought of how hard I come when you do...Christ, the reward is amazing." He held her to him as he rocked into her warming pussy. "I may come just from the thought of you biting me, love."

She licked his pulse and felt his cock jerk between them. He then lifted her up and turned so that she was sitting on his lap when he sat in the chair. Lifting her again, this time with him holding his cock, he lowered her over him until she was riding him.

"Christ, this is amazing. Lick me again and bite me. I need for you to bite me, Awnia. You can bite me anywhere and I'll love it." She nodded. The thought of taking his blood into her body made her restless, wet, and hot. The shifting of her teeth made her want him more, need him more than anything she'd ever needed. He pulled her tighter to his body, her clit touching his abdomen every time he moved. "Do it, love. Do it and I'll come inside of you again."

The moment she bit into his flesh, he roared. So much of his blood flooded her mouth that she had to swallow quickly twice, but knew that she still missed a bit. As she drank from him, he fucked her hard, bringing her body to his over and over. When he pinched her clit, her body bowed back from the climax that ripped from her. He lifted her up and took them both to the floor as he fucked her through four more earth shattering climaxes before he dropped on top of her. His own climax had been strong enough to have moved them both across the floor as he fucked her hard.

Awnia was weak from his passion and hers. When he finally lifted his head from her breast, she saw blood and pulled him to her to seal the wounds as she'd felt him do to her. When he looked at her again, she smiled at him.

"I think, my lady, that you have worn me out." He kissed her nose before shifting his body over hers so that his weight was beside her and not on her. "Someday we're going to slow down, but until then I'm going to enjoy you as much as possible."

"I hope we never slow. This is amazing." He pulled her body over his and held her. She knew that something was wrong, but also knew that asking him wouldn't get her anything. Instead of looking into his mind, she waited on him. She was nearly asleep when he spoke.

"My parents are on their way here. I know you're aware of that, but I wanted you to know that they hate me and will more than likely hate you as well when they find out we're a couple." Lifting her head from his chest, she looked at him. "They're going to try all sorts of things to get me to give them back the house and money, but I'm not going to do it no matter what. And I'm reasonably sure that they had something to do with a few other murders that I'm just remembering. Am I being a bastard for tossing them out?"

"No. I would never think that of you. People like that, they generally land on their feet again anyway." He nodded, and she lay back down. "My mother and your parents. Do you suppose we should put them in a ring and see who comes out on top?"

"That might work. Until your mother pulled out her magic." He lay there for a few seconds. "What is your mother's talent anyway? Your father said he was a builder. And then he showed me what that meant. Scary talented, by the way."

She giggled. "My mother's talent...besides making trouble...is sex." He lifted his head and looked at her. "She's a succubus."

"A goddess of sex?" Awnia nodded. "Christ, no wonder you're so good. I think...no, I don't even want to think about her and sex, but I'm betting you could give her a run for the title. You're very sexy, and make me crazy at least ninety million times an hour."

She lay there for several more moments, not really thinking of much of anything, when someone knocked at the door. Neither of them moved, knowing that the door was locked, but when Deacon spoke from the other side, they sat up and stared at the closed door.

"I'm sorry, my lady and lord, but there is something...would you mind coming to the kitchen? We have a slight problem." They were both scrambling for their clothing when he spoke again. "If you'd be so kind as to hurry, I'd very much appreciate it."

~~~

Samuel glared at Margo. She didn't touch him, but she did stand there looking at him while tapping her foot. Of all the places to get hurt, this had to be it. When the door opened again, not only was Deacon there, but Hawk and Awnia as well.

"Well shit." Margo hit him in the head with her towel. This was the third time she'd done that, and he wanted to take it from her and hit her back. But he wouldn't. His mother would have his hide if he did.

"Don't touch him."

As Awnia stood in front of him, he watched her face. He'd been running in the woods when something zapped him. When he'd woken, he'd found his way here, which was closer than going home. And now, he could remember very little about the incident other than it had made him puke up his guts for ten minutes before he'd felt he could move again.

"I don't feel well and I don't know what hit me." Awnia nodded and put her finger to his forehead. The pain that had been excruciating leveled out, became more tolerable. Samuel waited until she was finished before continuing. "I was my lion and running the property when I felt...it was hot, so I thought it was you. Then there was this pain that hit me in the back of the neck and seemed to curl up into my brain. That's all I remember until I woke up near here. Do you know what it was?"

"Yes." She went to his back, and Samuel looked up at Hawk. He asked him if he could tell Kennedy that he was fine. She wasn't believing him.

"Is she on her way here?" He told Awnia that she was. "Good. You're going to hurt more before you're better. Your son, will he be coming as well? I would say leave him at home where he can't see you like this and he'll be safer. But I don't think he's going to like being parted from you."

"Safer? What do you mean, safer? I don't...what the hell is wrong with me?" Awnia came to stand in front of him again. "Just tell me. I'm scared shitless now."

"My mother. She hit you with her magic. Not a great deal, but enough that she's marked you. She's taken a part of your mind that she can control, actually. I can remove it, but it's going to be painful. The good news is that she can't use her magic on you in this realm. She'd have to go home first. But I'm betting that she won't waste any time getting back there to try to control you. We're going to have to work fast, Samuel. She more than likely didn't know you were the leader of your pride and stronger than her, or you'd be dead about now."

"What do you need me to do?" When she looked at Hawk, Samuel felt his cat stir. He was actually glad to feel him, he'd been sort of quiet since he'd been hurt. "Awnia, I'd very much like to strangle you right now if you won't tell me what the fuck is going on."

"You're her servant. And as such, when she returns to her lair, she can order you to do anything." He started to ask her what that meant. "She will more than likely start with your wife and child, then move to your mother. After that, she'll have you in her complete control because of the devastation that murdering them will do to you."

"I won't kill my family." She sat down, not saying a word while staring him. "No one can make me do that. I'm not going to do that."

Awnia touched his hand and said a word. If he had to repeat it ever, he knew that he'd never be able to. But as soon as she pulled her hand back, he slapped himself in the face...twice. And hard enough to draw blood. When he reached for the knife that was lying on the table, he looked at her. She put her finger on the tip and looked at him.

"I'm not nearly as powerful as she is with this sort of magic, Samuel. But I could have you plunge that into your body over and over until you bled out. She will make you do anything she wants for as long as you live if I don't work fast. I'm only telling you this because what I have to do to remove it is going to be ten times harder on your body and that of your cat than what she did to put it there." He put the knife down, and she handed him a napkin. "When I take this from you, you're going to beg me to stop. You're going to try and kill any of us that keep you from the task that she gives you. You'll hurt like you've never hurt in your life. While you can, I need you to give me permission to take it out. And to let your friends do whatever it takes to keep you safe. I will need you to allow me to give you enough of my magic to save you."

"Yes, I give you permission to do whatever you need to do to keep me, and all the rest of us, safe. Anything. Just do it." He looked at Hawk. "You're in charge of me. Do you need anything? A written sheet of paper? Anything?"

"No. You've given me what I need." Samuel nodded and looked at Awnia. He had to ask her. And he had a feeling she knew he was going to.

"Can I die from this removal?" She nodded. "And if you leave it in, will my family die? You're sure of that?"

"Yes. If I were that diabolical, it would be what I'd do to you. You'd be at my mercy. A broken man without any will to live but what I give you." He nodded. "Samuel, I'm very sorry about this. I never meant for any of this to happen."

"Of course you didn't." He leaned back in the chair. "Just wait until Kennedy gets here. I want her here. I...I love her, and if I—"

"I'm not going to let you die if I can help it." He nodded. Tears burned at his eyes, and he nodded again. There was a good possibility, no matter what she said, that he was going to die from this.

"When I find your mother, I'm going to fucking tear her apart for this." Awnia nodded and he pulled her to him to hug her. "I'm so sorry, honey. I'm just really glad you're here to help me."

Kennedy came into the room just as he was letting Awnia go. She looked at him, then the rest of the room. When he stood up, hoping to take her somewhere to talk to her, she started sobbing. He pulled her into his arms as she started talking to him.

"*Tá tú ainmhithe balbh mór. Cad atá déanta agat anois? Ní féidir liom maireachtáil gan tú. Ní bheidh mé. An gcloiseann tú mé?*" He lifted her chin up and told her in English. "I called you a big dumb animal. And then asked you what you have done now. I can't live without ye. I won't. Do you hear me? Ye own me."

"I love you too much to leave you willingly. I love you with all my life, love. But Awnia is going to do everything in her power to save me." Kennedy looked up at him. "We have to talk, love. I need to tell you some things."

"Nay, you tell me now." He told her everything that Awnia had said and what had happened to get him here. Kennedy turned to Awnia. "I'll not threaten you with death if he dies, 'twill do none of us any good. But he's my life, you know. All I have in the world is in this man. I canna live without him. So I'm begging you, from a woman who loves her husband with all her heart to one that loves her mate as much, please don't let him die."

"I won't. But we have to hurry."

Samuel nodded. He moved to the doorway that led to deeper in the house. When he entered the living room, there stood all his friends, all his best friends, and he staggered just a little. He leaned on Hawk when he looked at each of them.

"I might die." Each of them nodded. "If I do, I'm asking each of you to care for my mate and family. They're all I have. You men...all of you are the best things that have come into my life besides my wife and children, and I can't think of a better group to help bring me through this than you."

He was led to a room on the second floor. Deacon and Margo were taking out all the breakables, and the bed was stripped clean of linens. At each corner was a thick chain. He knew then that he was going to be tied down.

Samuel moved like a man going to his execution, and a thought bubbled through his mind that he more than likely was. He was terrified and didn't mind admitting it. As he moved closer to the bed, his head felt as if someone had rammed a spike into him. He felt her then, this bitch who had hurt him, felt her telling him it was time for him to do as she said.

"She's starting. Hurry." Samuel felt himself being pulled. He looked at Kennedy and thought about ripping her throat out. But he fought it and screamed at them to hurry. The first chain around his wrist made his cat snarl.

The chains were holding him down, but he pulled anyway. Samuel tried to fight against the pain in his head, knowing it was the bitch, but she pulled him under. Twice he begged Kennedy to come to him, and when she wouldn't, he snarled at her.

You'll kill her. The voice rang in his head as if she were standing right next to him. And he could no more tell her no than he could have Kennedy. As he reached for her again, the most incredible pain took his breath away, and he screamed with it.

Every time he went down, his mind shifting to something dark, he knew that he said things. Not really sure of the words, but he knew that the words spewing from his mouth were not his thoughts. Still the pain raged on, the mind-blackening pain that took him under again and again. And still she was there. Shouting at him, screaming at him to bend to her will. And he wanted to. He needed to do as she said, and he tried so very hard to fight her.

Are you listening to me? I have the power to destroy all that you are. Kill the cunt. She's fucking every male in your pride; fucking kill her.

Samuel wanted to kill them all. Tear their throats out and destroy their bleeding bodies. His mind latched onto Awnia, and he knew that she was going to take this away, remove the voice from his head. Samuel screamed at her to leave him alone.

"Samuel, fight it." He heard her voice, the voice of the daughter. He snarled again and tried to shift. The need to claw her body apart, ruin every part of her, made him yank at the chains again. This time they gave a little.

He pulled and pulled on them. Time. The word, the concept kept at him. Time. Time. He was running out of it. And it was the daughter's fault. Samuel pulled harder on the chain as the pain made him sick. He threw up once, not even caring that he had. The first chain at his wrist was close to being free, and he yanked harder and harder still.

Free. His mind, and the woman, shouted with jubilation over it. As he reached behind him for the daughter, he felt his claws stretch and cut deeply. Satisfaction made him laugh. Even as he pulled hard on the other chain, the need to kill her was imminent.

A scream tore at his head. Not his...the scream wasn't his, but he liked it. Needed more of it. Clawing again, he felt heat. A flame had been set to his flesh, and his cat screamed as well. The pain in his head tripled, then doubled again as he tried to get away from it.

"Now." The daughter again. He reached for her just as he felt something shift again. His cat was there, but he was hurt, his breath laboring after something that had happened to him. As Samuel reached for him, tried to give him comfort, the woman in his head told him to kill it, to destroy the cat. Samuel tried to get him to come to him, for his cat to take his body so he would be stronger. But he lay there, not moving, as something seemed to pull at his mind again. This time he knew that he was dying. His cat was nearly there already.

Calmness settled over him. The thoughts of death, of killing, seemed to be leaving him. As he came back to himself, Samuel had a feeling that he'd run a great distance, that his body had been battered and beaten severely. His eyes, his entire face, felt like they had been burned by a torch.

"Samuel? Can you hear me?" Kennedy, his Kennedy. He tried to reach for her; the need to pull her to his body was overwhelming, and his heart was heavy with something he'd done to her. "Samuel. You need to rest now."

"I love you." He heard her cry and wondered about that for several seconds as he began to shut down, his body seemingly melting into a pile as he tried to fight it. "I love you," he said again as his mind blanked out.

CHAPTER 10

Awnia watched the big lion sleep. He was going to hurt when he woke, but he would wake. She looked over at his mate as she slept by his side. Awnia wondered if she knew how badly her mate had wanted her dead.

"Will you heal?" Awnia looked at Summer, who had come in to bring her some lunch. Hawk was sleeping on the floor at her feet. "He hurt you pretty badly. Will you heal soon?"

"I'll have to have Vinnie do it." She didn't ask, so Awnia didn't explain. But she did look at the wound.

Samuel had caught her when he'd been able to free himself. Hawk had tried to catch his hand, but he'd caught him as well, across the face. The wound in her leg was much worse. It stretched from her thigh to her ankle, and each of the four marks were at least two and sometimes three inches wide, and to the bone in several places. But she could no more heal herself than anyone of her kind. She almost envied Hawk and his ability to shift and become whole again.

"He's going to feel just horrible about that. Samuel would never willingly hurt another person, especially one that is helping him, for any amount of money or fame."

Awnia nodded at Summer. "I wish that there was something I could do to help you."

"I'll be fine." Vinnie had told her he'd return soon. That had been over two hours ago. He'd contacted her twice since then and told her that he'd been delayed by something, but he assured her that he'd be back.

"May I ask you something?" She nodded at the older woman. "Your mother, she's the cause of this, I get that. But why? I mean, why does she want you dead?"

"I can answer that." Her dad came into the room then and kissed her on the forehead. "I've never realized the extent of her hatred toward you until now. And for that I am truly sorry, my child."

"How could anyone hate their own child so much?" Awnia had no idea, but she had the feeling it was more than the fact that Temptress didn't like her father either. She waited for him to answer Summer. "She's such a lovely girl, and so nice to everyone. I'd be proud to have her as a daughter."

"I've been doing some research on her. And there is a bit you should know firsthand. It's about us, Temptress and me." Her dad looked at her. 'I'm so sorry, my love. Had I really known what she was about…or even that you were still alive…I would have done a great many things differently. Like first of all, I would have come for you."

Nodding, she let him tell Summer and Kennedy, who was awake now, what had happened to bring them together. As she sat there, she looked around the room and wondered if her life with Hawk would end any better.

I love you. Awnia looked down at Hawk when he spoke in her mind. *I love you with all my heart, and will forever.*

I've fallen in love with you as well. He put his hand on her injured leg, and she felt the warmth of him. *When Vinnie heals me, you'll be there, won't you? It won't be so bad, but it will look horrible.*

I've been talking to him. He's got some problems with some of the faerie in his realm. He's explained to me that you'll have to heat up again and he'll cool you off. But he said it won't be like before. You'll just be hot enough to heal. She nodded. *Will I be able to do what you can someday? Heat up like you do, maybe enough to heal you myself?*

I don't know. I really don't. I do believe you're my mate now, but I'm terrified to have you see. The bonding process is not pretty, and from my one experience with it, it's extremely dangerous. He asked her if it was more dangerous than what she'd done for Samuel. *Yes, but in a different way. This will involve you, and I can't stand the thought of you being hurt like Vinnie was.*

What does that entail? She shook her head, not wanting to tell him in the event that he tried it. But he must have read it in her mind because he smiled at her before speaking. *I won't. I promise you that. Not until you and I are both ready. I don't want to lose you any more than you do me.*

You have to absorb the part of me that no one else has touched. It's what the medallion holds. The witch gave it to me when I was ill. She told me that no one but my true mate would be able to take it into him. Awnia looked away when she thought of that time. *I think Temptress poisoned me. I'm not sure, and it has only just...when I was helping Samuel, I could feel her there. And while her mind was working elsewhere, I looked.*

How? How indeed. How could she have done that to her, and how had she gotten away with it? She looked at Hawk when he sat up and put his head on her lap, careful of the injury. *How did she do it?*

She had someone feed it to me. And then when I lay dying, she killed her as well. Loose ends, she called it. And the reason that everyone thought me dead was she simply made them believe it.

151

That I'd been buried as well. He took her hand into his. *She tossed me over the wall, as she had all the babes, but I somehow survived. Bringing the medallion with me.*

He stood up then and leaned down and picked her up as well. She hadn't realized how tired she was until she laid her head on his shoulder. Her leg throbbed, but having him hold her made it not seem so bad. As he took her to their bedroom, she noticed all the faeries in the hall. Yve landed on her hand as he carried her.

"We have a thought, my lady." Awnia yawned and smiled. "You are very tired, so I will make this quick. The fae and I, all the faeries, can heal you."

"No. I'm too hot for you." Yve nodded, then looked at the hand she was resting on. "Normally I'm too hot. With me being injured, I can still hurt you, but not as quickly. But I do thank you for—"

"We would still like to try. You have given us Master Samuel back in good health, and it would please us greatly if you would but let us try. We will start small at first to see if it will work." Awnia's mind was so tired she let her head fall forward twice as she was put on the bed. She thought she heard Yve say something like "thanks," but for the life of her, she couldn't think what she was thanking her for.

The bed moved, and she knew that Hawk lay beside her. When his arm curled around her waist, she put her hand over his and held him as she let sleep take her deeper. It rolled over her like a cloud on a lovely spring day.

~~~

The limo pulled into the drive at just after six. Hawk and Kaleb were sitting on the front deck, and Vinnie was in the yard with Stephen. The women were in the house making something for dinner, or at least thinking of something to order for dinner. Hawk stood up when the driver got out of the car to open the back doors. His mother practically leapt from the opening.

"That's far enough." She stopped moving and looked around at all the men that had seemed to suddenly appear from nowhere. He could count at least a dozen more than had been there before they'd pulled up. "I'm not sure what you're doing here, but I think that you've made your stance on our relationship pretty clear."

"Son? Why are you...do you think we could do this privately? Perhaps in the house?" She laughed a little fake laugh, and looked at him with a more fake smile. "I wasn't aware we'd be having company. I thought it would just be your father and I with you. And, of course, our cook and butler. How naughty of you to bring them here. We'll have to see about taking them back when we—"

"Since you weren't invited here at all, these men aren't here to be your company, but mine. They're mine and my wife's to be clear." His father got out of the limo then and came to stand beside his mother. "Father? You came too? That must have been pretty horrible for you, to come to see someone you abhor. What did she promise you if you came along? Or is it that you had no choice in the matter? That's it, isn't it? You're broke, and came to see what you could try and work out of me."

"She's my wife, and I go where she goes. And what's this I heard about a wife? You aren't seriously thinking of...Christ, you're not going to...does she know what you are?" Vinnie moved to stand beside him, as did Stephen. "These men, they look like well-bred men. What do they think of the kind of person you are? Do they have any idea what sort of monster is beneath that skin you have?"

"Frederick, please. You're not helping at all. I can handle this on my own." His mother looked at him when his father said nothing more. "We wanted to talk to you privately about this thing with the house and the money. You can't just turn us out like we're nothing to you. We're your parents. And I demand that you do this where we don't have to stand in the yard like common people."

"Common? No, you'd never think of yourself as something so mundane as common, would you, Mother? As for the house and money? I can and I did. Turn you out, I mean. Parents? You should look that word up before you go saying it like you have a clue. You haven't been my parents since you had that man Pruitt take me to that building and try to have the shifter in me taken out. By any means, you told him."

His mother paled and his father stood up a little straighter. "It might have worked had you not been so stubborn. One would think you enjoy being a monster." This time when his mother told his father to shut up, he told her to be quiet for once. "I'm not going to stand here and pretend that you're anything but a creature. A thing that has no business at all being able to live much like...you can't think you're going to have a child with a woman, do you? I mean, what if it turns out like you? Christ, the implications of that are just too fucking scary to think of."

"I think I'd enjoy that." Awnia came out of the house then, followed by Kennedy and Summer. Hawk noticed that Margo and Deacon were not far behind them, and neither of them looked like they were going to take shit from his parents again. "I'm Awnia, his mate. I'd like to say it's a pleasure to meet you, but I'm afraid that I have no desire to lie to you. In fact, I'd just like to say right now, you're a couple of assholes that have no idea what you're talking about."

"Good Christ, you're one too." His dad pulled his mother to him as he looked around the yard. "Do you have any idea what could happen if the two of you had a monster too? A shifter, they called him. A thing that can shift into anything it wants to. I just call him Monster. And if you have any sense whatsoever, you'll break ties with him now and get as far from him as you can. Well, before you get his sperm in you and have something as ugly as him."

"You mean like this?" Jimmy shifted, his big wolf taking him so quickly that from one heartbeat to the next it was over.

Next was Kaleb, who stood next to the snarling wolf. The big man grinned at Hawk's father as Kaleb pulled his shirt over his head. "I don't want to tear this. My lovely wife gave it to me for my birthday. She's breeding now, or she would be here too. And she'd no more take your shit than any of us. Meaner too, since she's carrying my monster."

As he stretched out, his big body covered in a dark fur before he was all claws and teeth.

The big black bear growled at Hawk's parents. As they screamed and ran to the car, Hawk noticed that their driver had also shifted, and stood as a great hulking panther in front of the door. They weren't going anywhere, it seemed.

"You think he's a monster, you should get a load of this." Vinnie let his dragon take him slowly. As he raised his arms to the sky, great wings spread from them as his body grew and expanded. His blue body took over his human one as his neck stretched out and teeth as big as the parents grew in his changing head. When he was complete, fully a great blue dragon, he snarled at Hawk's parents and blew a puff of hot air at them. Hawk laughed when his mother fainted.

His father dropped her on the ground as he came toward Hawk. "You think this is funny? That this is some joke? You bring these things here to what? Prove that you're not so freakish after all? Well, it won't work. I'm going to kill you myself." He looked at Stephen. "And you? What are you, pray tell? You can't possibly associate with these things as a human." Stephen only stood there.

The gun came from his father's breast pocket as he stepped up onto the deck. Before he could take it from him, Awnia put her hand around the barrel and stood in front of him. His father looked like he was frozen in place when Awnia started to speak.

"You're just going to piss me off if you shoot someone. And if you shoot me, you'll never live to see the end of the minute, much less the rest of your pathetic life." Hawk knew the moment that she'd started heating the gun when his dad whimpered. "That's right, I'm hurting you. And if you're very nice, I won't reach down and grab that tiny dick of yours and burn it off. As much as I'd very much like for you to not have any more children, I think you've already taken care of that, haven't you? Had a vasectomy the moment you knew what he was."

His dad nodded before he whimpered, then spoke. "It's her fault that he was even born. I was never going to have sex with her again, but she's very persuasive. He's her fault, I tell you. I have never had such a thing in my family line, ever."

Hawk felt his belly lurch up, but Awnia continued. "You think her the carrier of the gene that made Hawk? You're almost wrong. Nor did the hospital mess up the babies. You have the DNA that made him what he is, as does your wife. You both made him what he is. And do you want to know something else? His grandmother was a shifter as well. An elite, as he is."

"No." Awnia nodded and told him that he was very lucky to have him. "Lucky? You call it lucky to have such a thing as a child? Do you know how embarrassing it was to know that he could...? We tried to have it taken from him, but he wouldn't allow it. It was all we ever asked him to do, to go for this procedure to cure him. As a child, should he not have wanted to please us?"

"Procedure? Is that what you called it when someone chained him down and tried to take all his blood from his body while filling it with someone else's? Is a procedure when you drill into a person's head and try to see what abnormality is there so it can be removed? There was nothing they could have done to have 'cured' him. He is what he is because he's very special. To me and a great many other beings." Awnia looked back at Hawk, then at his father again. "I'm very glad he didn't cooperate with you on this. Because without him, I'd never be whole. Never have been this happy. You see, it's as much a part of him as my power is me. Would you like to know what mine is?"

"No." She laughed at him and let go of the gun. It was melted and sagging in his hand and his father dropped it. "I want to leave here now. I'll...we'll never come back here either. I don't want...I never want to see any of you again."

"I'm afraid it's not that easy. You see, I can read your mind, Mr. Hawkmen, and you have a great plan for your son. Your wife too, don't you? And I'm sorry, but I just can't let you do that." His father backed up when Awnia moved toward him. "I'm not going to kill you, but I am going to make you think every time you look into a mirror. I want you to know the pain and suffering you gave your son all these years."

"Don't."

Awnia nodded and blew at Frederick. Her breath, Hawk knew, was hot, hotter than a human might be able to stand. As his father dropped to the ground, Hawk came up beside her and held her while his father sat there.

"Tell your wife, convince her that bothering us again will be horrific for you both. And trust me when I tell you that you can't imagine what I can do to you if you piss me off."

Hawk's father looked at him. There was pain in his eyes, but also so much hatred that Hawk was startled by it.

"You monster. You fucking monster." Frederick stood up, his face so red it looked as if someone had painted it. "I'm going to tell everyone I know what you are. Tell them that a bunch of monsters live here and that you breed and have more monsters. I'm going to come back here with a hundred men with a hundred guns, and we're going to rid this earth of all of you."

His father picked up his mother, and Hawk watched them start to get into the limo. The driver was standing next to Kaleb and Jimmy. Hawk wondered if his father even knew how to drive. Then suddenly Stephen was there, lifting Frederick off the ground, his eyes blood-filled as he stared into Frederick's.

"When you think of this day, it will be a blur. Your scars will be a chilling reminder that will never reveal how you got them, the story too terrifying for your mind to comprehend. When you think of your child, your son, you will wet yourself in fear. Sleep will be disturbed. You'll sit in a corner so terrified that you'll beg for the light of day to end it. But it will never end. For each time he is mentioned, every time you read about him, you'll remember the fear over and over. You'll never tell a soul, do you hear me? You and your wife will leave here and never return. You'll do this or I'll hunt you down and drain you." Stephen let his beast go and shook Hawk's father. "Had I had my way, I would have taken you as high as I could into the sky and dropped you into the ocean. But I fear that the waters are polluted enough without you mucking it up more."

He dropped him then, stepped over his form, and looked at Hawk. With a nod, he left. Stephen would need to feed, his anger and the light of day taking a great deal out of him. The driver shifted back and pulled on his clothing. As he helped them into the car, he looked at Hawk.

"I should like to return. I've a need for a good leap, and this is a good one." He told him he'd have to talk to Samuel. "I'll take them to a hotel and set them up. I'm sorry, sir, but I have an idea that they're broke."

He gave the man all he had on him, then the others helped out as well. When David Harris left, he had enough money to cover his tab and to put Hawk's parents in a hotel for three days. He promised he'd be back. Hawk told him he was looking forward to it.

~~~

Samuel had missed it all. They were all in his room now telling him what had happened. He'd been taken to his own home, and telling him how much fun it had been to take care of Hawk's parents was funny, but a little disappointing. Samuel kept looking at Awnia. She'd not said a word since they came in.

"I'd like a word with you, if you don't mind." The rest of them were leaving, his mom running them off when he asked her to. Kennedy was still beside him, and he knew from her telling him everything that had happened when he'd been hurt that Awnia had also been injured badly.

"Kennedy tells me that the faeries were able to repair the damage that I did to your leg." She told him it was fine. "It's not fine. I hurt you. And badly too."

"Yes you did. But you were only hurt because of me, and I think that makes us about even. So if you don't mind, I'd rather not fucking talk about it." He nearly laughed at her. She'd never shown much in the way of temper before, and he loved it. "What the hell are you smiling about?"

"Do you have any idea how much I'd like to hug you?" She backed away. "I know you're not going to allow it, but I'm going to do it as soon as I'm up and about." He was weak...not as much as he'd been when he woke, but he was still weak. "Hawk said you took more of a risk helping me than you'd told us. Can you tell me if the faeries helped you with that too? I didn't know that they could do that."

"I didn't tell you anything, so how the heck would you know?" He nodded. "It was worth it. You're fine now, and things will be back to normal now. The faeries? Yve...I knew that they were capable of helping someone, but I'd never thought of it on the scale that they did it. Each of them gave...did you know that tear drops of a faerie are very powerful? I didn't. They had each saved a single tear from their happiness when you were saved. They put them on the wounds and they healed."

"I wasn't aware of it, no. But I'm glad they were able to help you. I understand that it was a very large wound." She shrugged. "You sure are very helpful when I ask you something, aren't you? Anyway. As for us getting back to normal, I'm not sure that's ever going to be possible in this pride. You saved my life. At a great risk to yourself. I can't thank you enough for that."

"Yes you can. I need for you to do something for me." He nodded. He'd do just about anything for her. "Hawk and I...we would like your permission to be as one. I won't let him try to be my mate...it's too dangerous for him. But if you could let us be together, things between us will be better."

"Better how?" She started pacing, and he looked at Kennedy. She was as confused as he was if the look on her face was any indication. "Awnia, how will things be better for the two of you?"

"My father believes that Hawk is my mate. I don't...you have no idea what would happen to him if he tried and failed to go through the process. I've seen it fail before, and I can't let that happen to him. But if you give us your blessing, so to speak, I can give him a part of me...not the mating part, but a part of me that will keep him safe should Temptress come. When she comes." Samuel waited for her to continue. And when she didn't, he did.

"And this other part of you, the part of you that is his mate, what is it? How is it different than the part of you that you're willing to share with him?" She continued to pace, and he looked at Kennedy again. *She's afraid of this?*

Yes. I think that she's more afraid of sharing with Hawk than she is her mother coming here. And she is coming. Yve told me just a little while ago. She won't be able to hurt you again either, she told me. That was news to him, and he was going to find out more later. *Help them.*

"It's my power. I have a great deal of it. Not just my heat, but...I can do things that will make our lives much better. All of our lives." He wanted to tell her his life was just fine the way it was, but she cut his thinking off. "You're never going to die, Samuel. Not ever. Neither will your wife or your children. Just after I helped you, I helped them as well."

"Never is a long time." She nodded. "Why would you do this without my permission? What gives you the right to—?"

"You did. I told you before I began that I'd have to share myself with you." Samuel wanted to be pissed, but she had saved his life. "I beg for you to allow me to give it to Hawk as well."

Samuel nodded. He wasn't thrilled with her doing this to him, but he wouldn't begrudge her giving it to Hawk. They deserved a long and happy life together.

After she thanked him and left, Kennedy stretched out beside him.

"Forever." He nodded. "We can have sex forever. And I'm thinking, we might need to have another wee one or two as well." He put his hand over her belly that was already swollen with their child. "You up for it, big boy? We're gonna need a lot of practice, I'm thinking."

He rolled her to her back and took her mouth. "A great deal of practice, I'm thinking." He cupped her breast in his hand and nibbled on the tip. She purred for him, and Samuel thought this living forever stuff might not be half bad.

CHAPTER 11

Temptress hated the body she was in. First of all, he was weak, and secondly…well, he was a male. As soon as they were back at the hotel, she lay on the bed and willed her body from his. Vega looked like he wasn't going to make it much longer. They'd taken a great deal from him.

"What did you do?" She moved to the mirror and looked at her hair. It was a mess again, and she wished she'd thought to bring someone with her to dress it. Rysdan was simply too— "I asked you what you did. Tell me."

"Tell you? I don't listen to demands from humans. But if you must know, I did nothing. You were the one that helped me get to him so that I could control him. Thank you for that." Vega struggled to sit up and she turned from him. His body was worse than they'd thought. He would be lucky to make it to the end of the day. "I merely told you how to do it."

"Control who? What is it you made me do, Temptress? Will I go to prison for this?" She looked at him in the mirror and showed him what he'd done. When he lay back on the bed, she smiled and turned.

The connection to the big animal was going to get her so much. First of all, she was going to have him kill for her.

Then there was the added fact that with her in his mind, she could finally get rid of that damned daughter of hers before it was too late. He was hers.... Vega whined again.

"Oh, don't be such a big baby. You were going to kill him anyway. This way we both get what we want. You have him out of your hair and all hope of the daughter having a mate is gone as well. Think of it as a win-win for both of us." He said something, but she didn't hear it. What did she care about his whiney ass? "Tomorrow, if you're still alive, I'll take you back to my world and have someone fix you up, and you'll live happily ever after."

"Did you hear me? I said that wasn't her mate." He sat up when she turned again. "Hawkmen doesn't use a cat as his animal. He uses a hawk. Thus the name. I would have thought that someone that is supposed to be as smart as you would have figured that one out."

"What do you mean, you got me to the wrong person?" Vega lay back down and put his arm over his eyes. "I asked you a question. If we didn't get the mate, then who did we get?"

"I have no idea. Some other shifter, I would imagine. And *we* didn't get anyone...*you* did. I was merely there." Vega looked at her. "So does this mean that the daughter is still going to have a mate? It would serve you right for what you've done to me."

"Done to you? I've made your miserable life a good deal better than it was. You can at least have sex now." He looked down at his stiff member. It was in poor shape as well. She and Rysdan had been using him for days now, even without his permission. But they'd been stuck here for days without any sexual relief.

"Yeah, that's worked out so well for me. How about for your next help to me, you cut off my balls. They're not much use to me right now anyway, as you never let me empty them. Or I have it. How about you just fucking let me go?" He started breathing heavily, as if he was having some difficulties. She watched him struggle, wondering what the hell she was supposed to do with him now. "You fucking cunt, I'm dying because you decided to use my body as a...as a vessel, and now, because you didn't take into account that I might not be able to handle it, I'm fucked. And do you want to know what else? I'm not going to live long enough to even enjoy half the shit you promised me."

"Nope, you're not."

He glared at her and lay back on the bed. Stupid man. Did they all think that everything was about them? More than likely. And he had been a sorry excuse for a vessel. She had thought, as Rysdan had, that with his black magic he'd be able to handle it. But she'd burned him up. From the inside out, as soon as she'd entered him from her pit to this realm. Getting her body out of his had been frightening at first. Then she'd noticed his cock was as hard as stone and leapt on him. Christ, it was the best fuck she'd had in a very long time. But now...now he was a shell of the man she'd used, and she was sick of his whining as well.

She left him then. There were things she had to do. Rysdan was in the other realm gathering supplies for them, as she couldn't return right now. Something about Halmar blocking her from entering. Temptress would take care of that as soon as she came into her power.

The daughter had to die. Temptress had had only three more children after she'd been born, and one after she'd dropped her into the hole. Temptress was terrified that the curse was coming to pass. And if it did, and the daughter came into her power, Temptress would lose it all.

"I won't." She looked around when she'd realized she'd spoken aloud. The witch had told her that a child, a single child, would destroy her. She'd even told her, in great detail, how it would happen.

She will be born with such beauty that you will pale greatly in comparison. Once she has come into her own, a mate to love her as no one will, life to be happy in as none she'd ever known, and friends to cherish her for what she means to them, not what she can give to them, she will be stronger than her sires will ever be. And loved by all that know her. Temptress had blown her off. Her plan had always been to kill anything that came from her body. And until that one time, it had worked so well.

Temptress was sort of worried about the lion that she'd taken control of. If he wasn't the mate, then who was he? If he was important, a lord or whatever they called the ones in charge in this world, she had broken a huge law. No, she thought, he'd been a shifter and running, so why would she have thought any differently? More than likely he was a nobody, not anyone to be concerned about. But at the back of her mind, she had a feeling this, too, was going to bite her in the ass.

She stood in line at the coffee shop. It was her newest addiction. Who knew there was such a wonderful thing as coffee? And those cream-filled thingy's were to die for...just too good to pass up. The list of the kinds of drinks were amazing too. Temptress had no idea what to order, so would just order the same thing that the person in front of her did. So far she'd been very lucky in that she'd loved each kind.

Her turn came and she did as she usually did, and put in an order for the sweet rolls by simply pointing to them. The man looked at her oddly but turned and ordered her the drink. Then when she moved along, Temptress caught a glimpse of herself in the glass behind him.

Something was happening. Turning to leave the café, she covered her mouth with her hand. Her lips were peeling open; the lower one was split deeply. The use of her magic here in this realm was taking away from her beauty and her energy. Running back to the hotel, she nearly fell twice. The heels that she'd gotten broke on one shoe, and she was left limping along. By the time she was pulling out her keys to get inside, away from staring eyes, she felt her cheek split open and her eye swell shut.

The key wouldn't work. It took her several minutes of crying in frustration to realize she was at the wrong door. By the time she was in the room, she was bleeding badly, and her body was beginning to sag. Something in her mind made her think this was the curse, but she shied away from that.

Vega was sitting on the side of the bed, dressed, which surprised her. For the past several days he'd only worn a sheet. But when he looked up at her, she could see the shock on his face. Covering herself as best she could, Temptress made her way to the bathroom.

"What the hell happened to you?" She didn't answer him as he shouted through the door. "You look like...well, hell you look like you're falling apart."

She did not need this right now and snapped her fingers. The magic that she meant to use on herself went to him and she heard him fall. As he did, the sound of him banging against something made her laugh, but a large chunk of her hair fell out. Fuck. She really was falling apart.

When Temptress came out of the bathroom, she had to step over Vega. He didn't look right, and it took her several moments to realize that his neck was bent at an odd angel.

When she listened for his heartbeat, she realized that he was dead. Sitting on the side of the bed, she just stared at him.

"Nothing is going right here." Her voice seemed strange, and she realized something else. Her sexy voice, the one she'd worked on for decades to perfect, was not there. The tears that she'd blotted at in the bathroom fell now, and she knew that her make-up, what was left of it anyway, was smearing.

An hour later, Rysdan came into the room. Temptress didn't even bother explaining to her when she asked what had happened. To be honest, and she seldom was, she wasn't sure where to even start. Nothing was going according to plan.

"I cannot bring you anything." Temptress looked at her helper. "There is a magical block on your rooms. I tried to bring through several things, but once I passed your doors, whatever I had in my hands was gone."

"Nothing?" Rysdan nodded. "There are things that I need. Now especially. Did you try that book, the spell book that I stole from the witch? It wasn't mine in the first place. That should be easy to get."

"It is no longer there either. A great many of your things are missing. I looked for those two charms you took as well, thinking we could sell them for this money that we need. They are not where you said you hid them." Rysdan sat down as she continued. "Even the clothing that you asked me to bring disappeared when I walked out of your rooms. And when I looked to see if they were back in the closet, they were not."

"Halmar." Rysdan told her she thought so as well. "What am I supposed to do now? He has made it so that I cannot go home. I cannot bring my things to me. How do I live? And where is he?"

"With the girl." Temptress shook her head. "There is a buzz about the kingdom about how he has his child back. Some are even speculating that you are dead and that this child, Awnia, will take your place. Halmar is taking her things as well. I think she has your books."

Temptress felt her anger rise. This shit was going to make it impossible for her to resume her role as a goddess. If this continued, Temptress had a real fear that the daughter would do just as the witch had said. Destroy her.

"We're going to her place. Where we were told by Vega that she was. I want to go there now." Rysdan didn't move. "Well? What are you waiting for?"

"You might want to check yourself out. I mean...I have no idea what is going on with you, but you're falling apart." Temptress growled. "I don't mind if you don't, but we have no money to speak of, and walking there is going to take us a long time. If you can do something with what you look like, perhaps we can get someone to take us."

"It is either we find her and destroy her with what I have left, or I look good. When she's finished, I will have everything back anyway." Rysdan stood up, but she didn't look like she was convinced. "It's going to be fine. I swear it."

"I thought once you destroyed the mate, that was going to end this." Temptress had a small shiver of fear settle over her. There was something there that worried her. The cat...who was the cat? "I'm taking it that it didn't work out."

"I have no idea. Are you coming or not?" They moved out of the room, and she had Rysdan summon them a cab. She had no idea how they were going to pay for it, but that would have to be low on the list. If she had to, she would make sure that he didn't charge for people to ride in his filth ever again.

~~~

Hawk touched his fingers to the soft wood again. He smiled when he heard the people behind him arguing. They could have waited for him to leave, but he was glad for the distraction. The desk he was working with was not happy with them any more than they were with each other. Well, the man who had owned the desk wasn't, at any rate.

"What will they do with my money, do you suppose?" Hawk said he had no idea. "Spend it on stupid things. Things that have no value once they get it. I've seen them toss out more food in the eight months I've been dead than we had for a year when I was growing up."

"People nowadays are very wasteful." He agreed. "I don't know what to tell you about your money. If you tell me, then I'll tell them. I'll even give them instructions on how you want them to spend it if you'd like." The man snorted. "I said I would give them to them, not make them carry them out."

"Do you know I'd have better luck having this desk that you're fondling do the right thing than the lot of them? More than likely they'll listen to you, nod those heads like that stupid plastic dog in the back of our car the missus and I had when we first wedded, and do what they want." Hawk had to stifle a laugh. "You laugh now, boy, but I'm telling you the truth. You have kids?"

"Not yet. I would like some, but we only just found each other." The man told him congratulations. "Thank you. My Awnia is very special. I'm very much in love with her."

"Awnia? What kinda name is that? Never mind. I don't care. What am I...what the hell are you doing now?" Hawk turned and looked at the man. His body wasn't formed, but

Hawk had been doing this long enough that he knew how to look. "Those drawers don't hold nothing them idiots need to find. Just some old pictures of me and their mother. Vacation and the like."

"They want me to tell them something. I can tell them whatever you like." He moved around the room, touching some of the items that had been left behind by a man who, for all intents and purposes, had led a good life. When he touched a small ceramic dog, he felt the connection to it immediately. "Your grandson."

"Yes. If I could tell him where it was at and have him manage it, I'd do it. But he's just eleven, and they'd take it before he could get it to the bank." Hawk put the dog back and picked up the small-framed picture next to it. "That's him. My pride and joy. Shitty parents, but he turned out all right."

Hawk started to put the picture back when one of the living relatives came into the room and moved to the desk, as far from Hawk as she could get. The tall boy beside her was sporting a black eye, and he looked like he would fall apart if someone said something to him. Hawk thought the boy looked depressed. As he walked by him, Hawk brushed against him and knew that the kid wouldn't make it if he stayed with this woman. He looked at the dead man.

"You know something." Hawk nodded once. "They hurting him? If they are, then I want you to take care of it."

"You know I can't." The man looked lovingly at the boy. "There is only so much I can do. I can...there is a way for you to help him if you'd like."

The man told him anything. After Hawk explained twice what he wanted done, the old man laughed. "This is going to be the best thing I've done since I made my first million. Get on with it. I'm ready."

Hawk nodded. "Mrs. Anderson, I've spoken with your father. He said there is no money at all. The desk that you're trying to sell is worthless, and as far as I can tell, there is nothing in it that he might have hidden."

"You're lying. That man was made of money. He'd never share it with any of us, but there has to be something." Hawk said nothing but looked at the young man. "I'm not going to stop looking. I deserve it more than anyone. I had to stay here the last five years with him. All of it should be mine."

"Yours?" The brother to the woman came into the room and snorted at her as he continued. "You only stayed here because you had nowhere else to go. You'd been kicked out of every other place you lived for non-payment of rent. And when Daddy decided that he wasn't paying them off again, you moved in here. I bet he just fucking loved that."

Just as he'd told him he would, the man moved the small dog. The movement was caught by the boy, but no one else seemed to notice as they argued. Hawk took it from him, making sure that the kid looked at him. When he did, Hawk nodded to the desk.

"You should have it." The boy looked at his mother. "It's for you. He wants you to have it."

"Me?" Hawk nodded. "You see him? You really see him? My grandda? Tell him that I miss him more and more every day."

"He misses you as well. He wants you to have the desk. He said that you and he had a great many conversations around it." The boy looked at the desk, then back at him. "Ask them. Your grandda is going to help you get it."

"I want him back more, but I'll take it." He told the kid to have a seat at the desk, and he moved to stand by the door to help if needed. Hawk had never done anything so underhanded in his life, but these people were hurting the kid and he deserved a chance.

"Mom, Uncle Denton, I was wondering if I could have this." He ran his hand over the smooth surface, and Hawk could see the boy's love for it. "It's not worth anything, and I'd really like to do my homework on it. If I have it in my room, I won't be bothering you at the table anymore."

The kid played it well, and it looked like their plan wasn't going to be needed. Then the woman looked at the man, and he knew that they were thinking how much money they could get for it.

"We'll sell it in a garage sale. Giving it to you will give us nothing, and if there really is no money, we need all we can get."

That's when the dead man made his move.

The drawers next to the kid opened first. The box of envelopes came spraying out of it so quickly that it looked like winter had settled in the room. The pens in the middle drawer were the next thing to go flying. Two of them zipped past the woman and her brother so hard that they stuck in the wall behind them. When they backed away from the desk, Hawk cleared his throat.

"I'm to inform you that if you don't let his grandson have the desk, he'll come to haunt you for the rest of your lives." The books on the wall started to come down. Not one at a time, but by the shelf full. "He said that if the desk stays with the boy, then he'll leave you alone."

"Tell him we will if he tells us where the money is." The chair next to her exploded, leaving padding and material all over the room. The woman stepped back, but Denton wasn't as quick and got hit by one of the legs. His screaming was enough to make Hawk wince.

"He said there is no money." She nodded as she helped her brother up. He was telling her to fucking give the kid the desk.

"What do we give a shit for? Do you want to be looking around all the time to see if he's going to try and kill us? I sure don't." Hawk looked at the boy, who was still at the desk. "If this doesn't prove to you once and for all that he's a fucking bastard, then nothing will. Give him the desk. But we're not paying you."

This last statement was directed at Hawk. Nodding once, he made his way to the desk. He'd help the kid carry it up to his room. He'd already heard they were going to live in the big house. About halfway up the stairs, with the help of two of the men in the house, the ghost man spoke to him again.

"He'll cherish this." Hawk told him he knew he would. "And he'll know when the time is right where the money was kept for him. I had already talked to the lawyer about setting it up so that my will wouldn't be read until he's eighteen. I'm going to take care of him when no one else would...and just let one of them try to hurt him again."

After he made his way home, feeling really good about what had happened, he reached for Awnia. She sounded happy as well, and told him what she was up to.

Halmar, my father, has brought me some things from his home. He told her that was wonderful. *I know. We are sorting through some of the treasures that he has collected. He has been to every place I've been.*

You and he are a great deal alike. He felt her joy at that. *I'm on my way home. And then I thought that the two of us would go out to dinner. Have a date.*

A date? We are already sleeping together, Hawk. A date seems silly. Fun, but silly. He liked that she was still happy, and thought the date sounded fun. *I have nothing really to wear out to see people. All my things are mostly what Kennedy calls casual.*

You wear casual very beautifully. I'll be home soon, and when I get there, we'll make a trip to the mall first. How does that sound?

Wonderful. He told her he loved her and closed the connection. To have a date with her was perfect. He'd ask her to marry him after they ate, and then figure out the soonest that it could be arranged. Hawk found himself whistling as he drove up the long drive.

CHAPTER 12

Halmar was nervous. He'd never done anything so...well, he hated to admit it, but underhanded in all his life. He should have been able to talk to the young shifter, but he'd called in Samuel to help. The big lion had agreed to help him much quicker than he'd thought he would.

"He's going to be all right." Halmar nodded. "You're sure about this? You think he's her mate and this will work?"

"I am. And he is. There is no reason to believe otherwise. She is in love with the man. Anyone can see that." Samuel nodded. "And when I spoke with Vicente, he said that while he loved Awnia, they both knew that they were not mates. This just feels right."

Samuel nodded. Halmar was wondering how much longer it would be until Hawk arrived home when he opened the door from the garage. Halmar could tell that he was suspicious, but he only asked where Awnia was.

"Kennedy and the others came to get her to go shopping. She said something about you and her going out tonight, and I asked Kennedy and Summer to take her. The others went along as well. Halmar and I need to talk to you."

Hawk nodded and asked if they could go to the living room. As they made their way there, he told them about his day.

"Will he inherit it all?" Hawk told him that he would. "And this mother of his, you say that she hurts him?"

"I don't think she'll be able to any more. His grandda said he was going to stay with him until he no longer needed him. I'm thinking the boy will need him forever." Hawk sat down, and Halmar wanted to pace. "You have something to tell me?"

"She's your mate." Samuel groaned when Halmar blurted it out. "I mean, she really is. And the sooner you get this process over with, the sooner she can be safe."

"I think you should have let me tell him." Halmar wasn't one to beat around the trees or whatever shrubbery they used. But Samuel asked him to have a seat and he'd explain. But young Hawk spoke first.

"She is my mate. I've been telling her that for weeks now. I have no idea what this process is, but if I can make it true, then I'd like for you to tell me."

"It's not as simple as that. You have to accept her. And trust her." Hawk nodded at Samuel, but he raised his hand. "It's not like that. You can't just say it, Hawk, but truly do it. Then when you find the piece of her that she's held onto, then you can be her true mate."

"You mean this?" Halmar watched as Hawk dug something out of his pocket. When he laid it on the table between then, he nearly laughed. The boy had it all along.

"Where did you get that?" He told him that Samuel had given it to him when he helped search for Awnia. "And you've had it all this time? Have you worn it? I mean, around your throat?"

"No. It's been in my pocket. I meant to give it back to Vinnie. He asked me for it a couple of times, but I found I just couldn't part with it. What is it?'

Halmar wanted to hug Hawk, but needed more information first.

"It's her. I mean the part of her that's reserved for her mate. It's supposed to contain a part of her heart, the part that beats." Both Samuel and Hawk looked at him oddly. "I'm not explaining this well. Let me tell you a story."

"Will this bond us?" Halmar nodded at Hawk. "If you tell me how it works, then I'll do it. I don't care what it is."

"When she was...she died. Or so we were all told. I never thought of it again. I never...it was only days before her sixteenth year, and she was supposed to come to her own then. But when she fell ill, the witch came to find me and told me she was born for great things. I, of course, knew that, but she said that if and when she found her mate, the gift to him would be gone because of the illness that nearly took her life. But that she could save a part of it for her and keep it safe." Hawk asked what it had been. "Like I said, a part of her beating heart. It's in that."

Hawk picked up the medallion and held it to the light. For anyone else, it just looked like a ruby red stone that sparkled around the room. To Halmar and the one that held his daughter's heart, it would look as if it pulsed. Which, of course, it actually did.

"I thought it was alive the first time I saw it." Halmar's confidence that this was the right thing to do grew. "She never...I touched it to her once. I thought for sure she was going to make me give it back, but she never asked for it. I don't think she knows what it is."

"She does." Hawk nodded at him as he put the medallion in his pocket. "She has no hope that you're the one. Or she's afraid to believe it. Her mother told her that she'd never find you. And I'm sure that she thinks, and I believe it as well, that her mother will destroy you before you can take her."

"We think that's what happened to me that day. Her mother came to find you, because according to Halmar, she is aware of you, and tried to kill me. With her mate dead, Awnia wouldn't be able to fight against her mother, and Temptress would win."

Halmar watched the young man. He was terrified, if he was honest with himself. If this wasn't her mate then all would be lost, because he knew for a fact that Temptress was here. And not just here, but coming soon to find and destroy his child.

"How will she destroy Awnia? She thinks she can, so there must be a way to do it. How?" Samuel looked at him. "Halmar, I'm going to ask Awnia to marry me tonight. And when she says yes, I want to spend the rest of my life with her. To do that, you're going to have to tell me what the fuck is going on."

"To destroy her, to end her life, she will kill you. And in doing so, Awnia's heart, the part you hold and the part that beats within her chest, will stop. If that happens, Temptress will take all that she is, much like how magic works. Only this will be more than this world can take. She will not just destroy Awnia, but every living creature in this world as well."

"By her fire." Halmar nodded. "And if Awnia wins...when she wins, what will happen to Awnia? Or better yet, her mother? What happens to Temptress?"

"Her age will show first. And it won't be easy either. Each year of her life will come to her; every hurt, every pain that she's had will be put upon her. Any harm that she's caused to others during her lifetime—our children and the people that she killed—will be suffered upon her. Each one of those will not be quick. Their deaths will play out in the way that she inflicted them." Hawk watched him, and Halmar knew that he had to tell him all of it. "Her magic, what she has left, will go to Awnia. And to you as well."

"There's more. What is it?" Halmar had hoped that he'd just be pleased with what he'd already told him. But he should have known better. The boy was sharp.

"She'll take her place in the kingdom. She'll...Awnia will be a true goddess." Hawk got up to pace. "You and she will need to come to our realm. Live there among your own kind. You could come here to visit, to stay for a time, but it will no longer be safe for her to be here unprotected. And the two of you will need to be protected."

"Why?" Halmar got up to pace as well. Hawk stared at him as he made two passes by him. "Halmar, I have a feeling that we're running out of time. Say it."

"She is the last of our kind. To have a mated pair of gods is so rare that we've not had one since...Temptress and I were the last. If you do not come to the realm and have children there, where we can keep them safe, then our world will die."

"Does Awnia know this? All of this?" Halmar shook his head. "Then you will tell her before I accept this responsibility. I will not trick her into anything. If she doesn't want to go to your realm, I'm just as happy to live and love her here."

Halmar started to argue with him, but Deacon came in the room.

"Sirs, there was a being at the gate. She had come through it before I could have it opened, had I wanted to, and is now on her way here. I have summoned Miss

Kennedy and the others home. Master Stephen and Lady Clar are bringing them here now."

Halmar looked at Hawk to plead with him once again.

"No. You tell her, or there will be no bonding or whatever you call it. I won't lie to her or make a decision for her. She will know as much as you do or it's over." He started to walk away, and Halmar looked at Samuel. He knew then there would be no help from him. The man was practically beaming with pride.

~~~

Awnia watched as her mother and Rysdan came toward them. Awnia felt her body heat up with anger that Temptress couldn't just leave them alone. Who was Awnia bothering by being here? No one.

"You're not welcome here." She smiled at Hawk when he stepped off the deck to stand in front of Temptress. "Why don't you haul your nasty self back to where you came from and leave us alone? No one here wants a thing to do with you."

"Do you have any idea who you are addressing? I am Temptress, goddess of—"

Awnia nearly burst out laughing when Hawk cut her off. "Yeah, a goddess. So what. I don't care who you are or what you think you might be. I have a vampire, a bear, a lion, a wolf, and a dragon here that don't give a fuck who you are either. So as I said, get on back to where you came from." Temptress took a step in his direction, and Awnia stepped beside him.

"This is your mate?" Awnia was shocked by her question. Not what she'd asked, but that she claimed that Hawk was her mate. He really was her mate. "He's nothing."

"I think he's everything." Awnia looked around. "These people have come here to protect me. But I'm pretty sure that I can take care of you myself, can't I? Your magic is all but gone. And we both know why, don't we?"

"I am your sire. I…this man, this being, will not be your mate. I will not have it. I have told you before, daughter, that if you find one, I will destroy him."

"Like you tried to do to the male of his pride?" Awnia knew that Temptress was afraid now. She'd not known that she'd hurt a male. Killing a leader of any creature was against their laws. It was the same as trying to kill one of their own. "Samuel is only alive because I took you from him, the evilness that you put into his head. You would have killed his family, his pride, had you defeated him. Do you have any idea what his kind would do to you if they knew?"

"Like I care at all what some shifter thinks about what I do or don't do." But she did, and everyone there knew it, Awnia would bet. Samuel came to stand beside her and Hawk, and Temptress backed up. "He doesn't look any worse for wear. Perhaps you lie about this. Just to make me look bad."

"You've done that all by yourself. Looking bad…looking really bad seems to be what you do best. And I don't lie, unlike you." Temptress moved Rysdan in front of her, and Awnia smiled. "She has not the power to do what was done to the male. You know that as well as I do. And I told you, I took you from him. I know it was you."

"Lady Awnia, you mustn't think that I did anything but follow her rules. I'm not a bad person. I was just following her commands." Rysdan dropped to her knees as she continued. "I will serve you, my lady, for all time if you would spare me."

"No." Rysdan looked up at her as if she hadn't heard her. "You will not serve me...you'll not serve anyone. You are to be held over in accordance with the laws of our kind. Halmar will return you to the cells where Temptress found you."

As soon as she disappeared, Awnia took a step closer to Temptress. She wasn't afraid any longer. The time she'd spent with her father was coming back to her. The rules of their kind. The punishment of each crime. Temptress would never leave this world alive, but she would suffer greatly when she was no longer living.

"I'm going to enjoy killing you. You're nothing right now. You will die and I will rule."

Awnia knew what she had to do as Temptress continued, backing away as she spoke. When she was backed as far as she could get her, Awnia turned and looked at Hawk.

"You are my mate. My love. My heart. I give to you the piece of me that no other being will ever have. I entrust to you all that I am and all that I will ever be." The pain in her back had her look at her chest. The knife protruding through it made her ache and drop to her knees. "Russel Hawkmen, take what I offer you."

She saw her father move. The pain was taking her breath way, and she turned her head to look at Temptress. The look on her face was of joy. She thought that she had won. Going to her hands now, Awnia looked at Hawk. Her vision was blurring when she saw him take the medallion from his pocket and put it over his heart.

"I accept."

The power lifted her from the ground. She heard Temptress screaming, but not what she was saying. Her body burned with power, her heart pounding as it seemed to overwork with her blood. When she felt as if she might explode from it all, she was lifted higher still and felt arms wrap around her. Hawk held her as they were pulled into a heated vortex.

"I have you." His love wrapped around her as if they had been created to hold her. As they lowered to the ground, sparks of magic surrounding them and falling to the ground, Hawk kissed her, touching something so deep within her that she knew that he'd love her forever.

Their feet touched the ground and still he held her, his mouth fused to hers. When he lifted his head, his smile gave her the most amazing feeling. Love. She knew what it was— pure love.

"You think this changes anything?" They both turned to Temptress. "It changes nothing. You're still going to be destroyed by me."

"I think not." Hawk put out his hand and touched it to Temptress's forehead. She stiffened and tried to pull back from him, but it was as if she were being held in a bond. When Hawk took Awnia's hand into his, she knew through the connection that he was holding Temptress, and that everything she knew, all her memories, were being transferred to them. And none of them were good.

When she dropped to her knees, Hawk let Temptress go. She sat there for several moments before she looked up at them. There was nothing left in her. She looked as if she'd been drained, which Awnia supposed she had.

"I hate you."

For some reason Temptress's admission of her hatred for Awnia hurt her. Awnia knew that she had hated her all along, but to have it said aloud made it all the more real. Awnia had spent her entire life, decades and decades of her existence, on the run from her or someone she'd sent for her.

But it still hurt her. There was no way now that she'd let her know.

"I've no love for you either. We've never been...I was going to say close, but had not Halmar found me when he did, you would have killed me as well." Temptress nodded and smiled. "You're going to pay for those crimes. You'll relive them all."

"They'll be but fond memories to me." She stiffened then, her back becoming ramrod straight and her arms stretched from her side. "They begin now. The first babe I tossed away. How it screamed as it fell to its death."

Awnia knew that, despite all she'd said, they were not fond memories for Temptress. The pain etched across her face said all that she was feeling...pain, horror, and even the last breath taken by the child. Over and over she felt it, each one a flash of harsh pain across her face. Suddenly, Halmar was standing in front of them.

"That's enough." When he moved, Temptress was gone. In her place was a circle of burnt earth that Awnia knew nothing would ever grow on again. Kneeling down to touch it, she felt not heat as she had expected, but cold. The ground was ice cold.

"As her heart was." She looked up at Halmar. "You should not have to witness her death. It is bad enough that she thinks this but a joke. I have sent her to the pit to die."

"Thank you." He nodded and walked away. Awnia leaned into Hawk as they stood in the yard alone. "You were right."

He laughed. "You'd probably do well to remember that I am always right. On most things, anyway."

Hawk continued to hold her until Yve came to them. She bowed low, then smiled when Hawk put out his hand for her. Another bow, and she looked around.

"The faerie would like to know if you will need them today. There is a matter of your magic, my lord and lady." Awnia asked her what she meant. "They have...there is...your magic is very powerful, and they wish to...they need to.... They wish to have sex."

Awnia tried her best not to laugh. Yve was blushing so red that she was sure that the reddest rose paled in comparison. Hawk, however, was not even trying, and he was laughing hard enough to shake the poor faerie.

"I have no problem with that. I'm curious as to why—"

Yve put up her hand and incredibly, her face heated more. "Do not ask me for details. We will have a profusion of babes born in a few weeks, and I will have to assign them work when they are ready to leave their nests." She growled low at Hawk when he laughed harder. "We already have over a hundred faerie to each plot of ground. They are to keep the flowers safe, water them with dew in the morn and night. There is barely enough work for them all to keep busy. I will have more than...what am I to do with them all?"

"Send them to our realm." Awnia turned when Halmar spoke beside them. "I can take as many as would like to go back with me. Can you have them ready in a few hours?" Yve nodded and thanked him. She was gone in seconds.

"You're going back?" He nodded at her, and Hawk walked away. "I thought you'd stay for a while. At least some time for us to visit."

"I must return and see to her." Awnia nodded. "But you...Hawk and you must come to live with us. There is no safe place for you here. Especially when you have children of your own. They will be sought after by all kinds of beings, simply for the little magic they are born with."

Awnia wanted to go home. To her home in the other realm. But she knew that leaving here would be hard on Hawk. He had so many friends here. His life was here. When Halmar said her name, she looked at him. He stared at her intently, as if he were looking deep within her.

"I'll speak with Hawk." He smiled and nodded. "I don't know what's to happen to us if we go there. I've no…there is nothing really there for me but you. I know no one, have no friends. I'm not even sure of the magic that I have now."

"You have a great deal more than either of us had to give you, I can see that now. Combined with your own magic, I would say that you're stronger than any other demi-god in our realm. Having a mate, one such as Hawk, has also given you a great deal more than we would have thought. You're very powerful. More so than I had…. If you stay here — and I hope that you'll think of coming with me — you could…I believe that the two of you could keep your children safer than we could."

"I do as well." He looked at the couple on the front deck. Samuel and his mate were leaving as well. "They have some of my magic too. I wonder if they know how much rained down on them when Hawk and I came together."

Everyone that had been in the yard when they were floating above them was sprinkled with magic. Even the child of Samuel was glowing with it. She looked at her father, Halmar, when he didn't say anything, but only stared at Samuel and Kennedy.

"They will be happy, I think, with the results of today. They are a couple deeply in love, and this will…this will only deepen their love for each other." Awnia told him of the faeries. "Ah, so that's what she meant when I happened upon you. I will take them back with me. There is a great shortage of magical beings such as them. I wondered for a long time if Temptress had anything to do with that."

She had, but Awnia didn't say anything to him. Temptress's memories were hers now. Every deed, small or large, was there for her to see. And Awnia knew that there was going to be a lot of work done in order to restore some of the things that had been nearly wiped out because of her.

As they made their way to the house, he told her what he was taking back with him and some of the things he would send her. Awnia was only half listening to him, and when he left, she went to find Hawk.

CHAPTER 13

"Did your father get away all right?" Awnia nodded at him, and Hawk noticed that she seemed to not be paying attention to him. "He said that when he gets back he's sending you a unicorn to ride. We'll be the hit of all the kids in the pride with one of those."

"I suppose." He nearly laughed, but decided to have some fun with her until she got whatever was on her mind straightened out.

"What about the statue of him? He wants us to put in in the front of the house with a large plaque with his name on it. I was thinking that it should say something like…Halmar the Magnificent. Then there are the pots of coins. Do you suppose they'll be gold? I'm kind of partial to gems myself. They're much more colorful and have such a nice shine." Still nothing. "And the trees that when shaken leave money in their wake. I don't know about you, but I'm thinking that it might need extra protection. Not the condom kind of protection. We'd want that to make as many little money trees as it wants. Perhaps we could sell them. How much—?"

"What the hell are you talking about?" He burst out laughing, and she glared at him. "What do you mean, money tree? And condoms? Are you on something?"

"Yes. I'm in love with you and it makes me sappy." He pulled her into his arms. "What has you so upset? Is it your father leaving?"

"No. He said that he'd be back." She looked up at him. "He didn't tell you he'd give you his tree, did he? He loves that tree a great deal, and to share it with you is a great honor."

"He has one?" When she grinned at him, he smacked her on the bottom. "You had me there for a moment. Now, tell me what's wrong."

"Do you want to go to the other realm?" She pulled away, and he let her. "We'd be...well, treated like gods if we went. There would be no need for us to do anything at all. Everything, including our food, would be made for us. I've just learned how to make a proper cup of tea. Though Kennedy calls it a cuppa for some reason. And all the things that I can learn. Summer is teaching me to knit. Knit. I've never had anyone show me that before."

"Awnia." She looked at him and he could see the excitement in her face, and knew it was for the idea of learning something new rather than going back home. "We can stay here. I have no problem with that. Samuel said that we could stay for as long as we want. By the way, he's sort of pissed about the magic stuff. He just figured out that he can move between his house and ours with just a thought. He showed up naked in our kitchen an hour ago."

"I bet that was a sight." Hawk nodded. "I want to go, but not forever. And as I said before, forever is a very long time. I think...I would think that you'd find it boring compared to all this."

Hawk made his way to her. They were in his work shed, a large barn really that he stored his cars in. He'd been talking to one of them when she'd come to him. The cars were not all that thrilled about him leaving either. They had told him if he left them again to lay rot and die, he would have to live with himself over it. Cars were not all that sympathetic.

"Nothing is boring where you are." Awnia smiled up at him. "You're beautiful, have I told you that lately?"

"Just about two hours ago when you left to come down here. Which, by the way, was only supposed to be for a few minutes." He had lost track of time. "And there I was, all naked in the bathtub, thinking that at any moment you'd come into the bedroom and find me all wet and clean for you. I was very disappointed."

"I can't have that." Hawk picked her up, and she wrapped her legs around him. "What about me not coming to you disappointed you first? The fact that I didn't get to kiss you?"

He did that now, tasting her need. Sitting her on the work bench he'd had made just for his tall frame, Hawk stood between her legs and rocked into her. He started to unbutton her blouse as he told her what he was going to do to her.

"I have a chair that I sit at when I'm working here. It'll be the perfect height to pull here and feast on you. Eating your pussy until you come so many times that you'll beg me to stop." Her moan had him tearing a button lose. "I need to taste your breasts, suckle at your nipples while I fuck you."

"Hurry." Another button went flying, and he couldn't wait any longer. Ripping the rest of them from her, he tore open her bra and took as much as her warm flesh into him as he could. Working at getting her pants off, he finally had to take a step back. "You need help?"

Nodding at her, he watched her shimmy out of the pants and nearly whimpered when she lay before him in just her panties and torn shirt. When she reached for his pants, Hawk took another step back.

"If you free me, I'm going to fuck you. And as much as I can't wait to be buried deep inside of you, I really want to eat you." When she nodded and leaned back, Hawk took a few moments to appreciate the glory before him, and he decided that there was not a luckier man in the world than him. Reaching blindly for the chair, he rolled it to him and sat down. Her pussy was so wet that her juices were staining the wood beneath her. He rolled forward and licked her from gate to clit.

"Please." Her scream of a plea had him smiling, and if he wasn't so needy right now, he might have teased her a little bit. But he wanted her to come, wanted to drink from her while she did so. So he slid his fingers into her sheath as he suckled her clit hard.

The sound of her scream was muffled by her legs tightly around his head. He continued to taste her even as she tried to pull him from her. He was determined to have his fill. Hawk drank her through another, then a third climax before he stood up. Christ, he was so hard that he felt as if he would shatter if she touched him.

"I'm going to fuck you." She whimpered again and reached for him. "No. Christ if you touch me, it's over. I'm coming over you instead of in you."

He stripped the zipper from his jeans as he pulled free of them. His shoes were thrown behind him as he kicked them away and he moved to her, holding his cock. Her nipples were small stones on her full breasts, a sheen of dewy sweat glistened on her body, and her legs were wide, her pussy showing for him. Hawk slid the tip of his engorged cock into her.

"I need to fuck you." He slid just a little deeper. "A hard, fast fuck that leaves us both sated but needing more."

"Yes." He moved his cock deeper still and put his hands on her hips when she continued. "Fuck me, Hawk. Now, please fuck me."

He slammed forward, his cock buried to the root. As he pulled free again to take her, she wrapped her legs around his hips, and her hands dug into his shoulders. He watched her face as she looked him in the eyes. Hawk felt a connection so tightly bound to her that he knew the exact moment when she came. And fucking her hard, he joined her when she screamed out her release.

~~~

Making their way to the house, she held his hand in hers like it was a lifeline. She supposed it was in a way. She loved him, and needed him more than she did anyone else. When they entered the kitchen, they were told to have a seat as lunch was served. Margo put a large plate of food in front of both of them. Awnia looked up at her.

"You might thank me for this later. That father of yours…he sent you some things to go through. I had Deacon put it in that room your daddy had when he was here. Did you know that he moved it around a bit? What was he thinking we'd do with it all?" Awnia wanted to go look now, but Margo only pointed to the plate and said to eat. She knew better than to argue with the woman. She glared at Hawk next. "And you. You should see what that lawyer sent over for you to look over. Those people that raised you — and I refuse to call them your parents — were into about everything. She said she'd be on call for the next three days just for you. I bet she's not free either."

"She and I have something worked out." Hawk was sort of nervous, Awnia could tell. But he finished his lunch and even took a part of hers. When he stood up, he put out his hand. "We'll see what mess you have first, because I'm sure mine is just a lot of reading. Then we'll tackle mine. You can help me decide what we keep and throw out."

She nodded and followed him to the back bedroom. Her father had been staying there when he'd visited, and she could see where he'd made some improvements. She had to laugh when Hawk stopped right inside the room.

"The room is not this big." She laughed harder when he started to pace off the room. "I'm pretty sure that this room alone is as big as our house. How the...? I'm not even sure I want to know how he did it. Do you think he'd mind if we asked him to do this to our room?"

"I'll ask him." There was a bump on the floor above them, and she grinned at Hawk. "Or maybe we'll just go and check it out later. I think he mentioned that when we're in this room, we have a direct line to him. We should be careful what we do in here."

Hawk nodded and picked up a large book. "What's this? It looks...I can read this. I know it's not in any language that I've ever learned. It looks like a book of spells."

She took the book from him and looked it over. "It is. It says that it was written for the goddess of magic. I wonder why Halmar...my father might have given this to us. I mean, this should be with him, at least."

Awnia set the book down when she saw a small stuffed animal. It was a unicorn, and she showed it to Hawk, laughing. "Did you put this in here? It looks old, but I thought you were trying to prove a point from earlier."

"No. I've never seen that before." She handed it to him when she saw a bed across the room. "It's yours. It says here 'for my darling daughter on her fifth birthday.' This is from your father."

She took it from him and held it to her nose. The memories came flooding back to her then, and she smiled at Hawk. It had only taken that small scent to take her back to being that young again.

"We were going to have pudding, my favorite. The kitchen had been working on it all morning, and I spoiled the surprise by going in when they were dishing it up. I can't remember why I'd gone in there, but they were so disappointed. I remember telling them that I loved them very much for doing this for my papa and me."

He hugged her to him, and she turned again to the bed. She wasn't even sure why she thought it was one, but knew that she had to see it. As she pulled some of the larger boxes from around it, she realized it was a crib. Her crib. Hawk wrapped his arms around her as she stared down at it.

"He told me when I was younger that someday I'd fill it with my own children. Father told me that it was magical and that all I had to do was tell my child that I loved them and the crib would cradle them in love." She leaned down and put her hand over the small pillow and blew across it. "Watch."

The bed began to rock gently, swaying back and forth in a slow movement. The designs on either end came alive then, the small animals seemingly pulling from the wood and beginning to dance above it. The animals, some of them real to this world, others only to her own, played in grass and low sunshine until it faded to night. Then as they moved to their beds, clouds of grass, bales of hay, and even a branch from a tree, the sky above them darkened to a lovely hue of blue with thousands of twinkling stars above.

"I remember this bed, even though I've not slept in it for so long. It gave me hope, fueled my dreams, and made me realize how much more was out there beyond Temptress's room and my father's." Awnia turned in his arms. "I want a child with you. Maybe as many as a dozen, but I want one soon."

"I'd like that as well." He cupped his hand over her belly. "I'm not sure how it works with us now. Before, you'd go into what we would call heat, and then you'd get pregnant that way. It would happen several times a year, but only once after we have our first child."

"We need only to decide that we want one." He picked her up in his arms. "Is this a yes? Do you want a baby as well?"

"Oh yeah, I want a child with you. And as many as you want." He carried her out of the room and up the stairs. "I just hope your father left the bed where it was. I'd hate to have to go looking for it at a time like this."

She was still giggling when they entered. Yes, her father had fixed their room, but the bed, a bigger and thicker one, was right near the door. Hawk dumped her on it, then started to strip her down. Life with this man was never going to be boring.

Available Now
The Entire Samuel's Pride Series

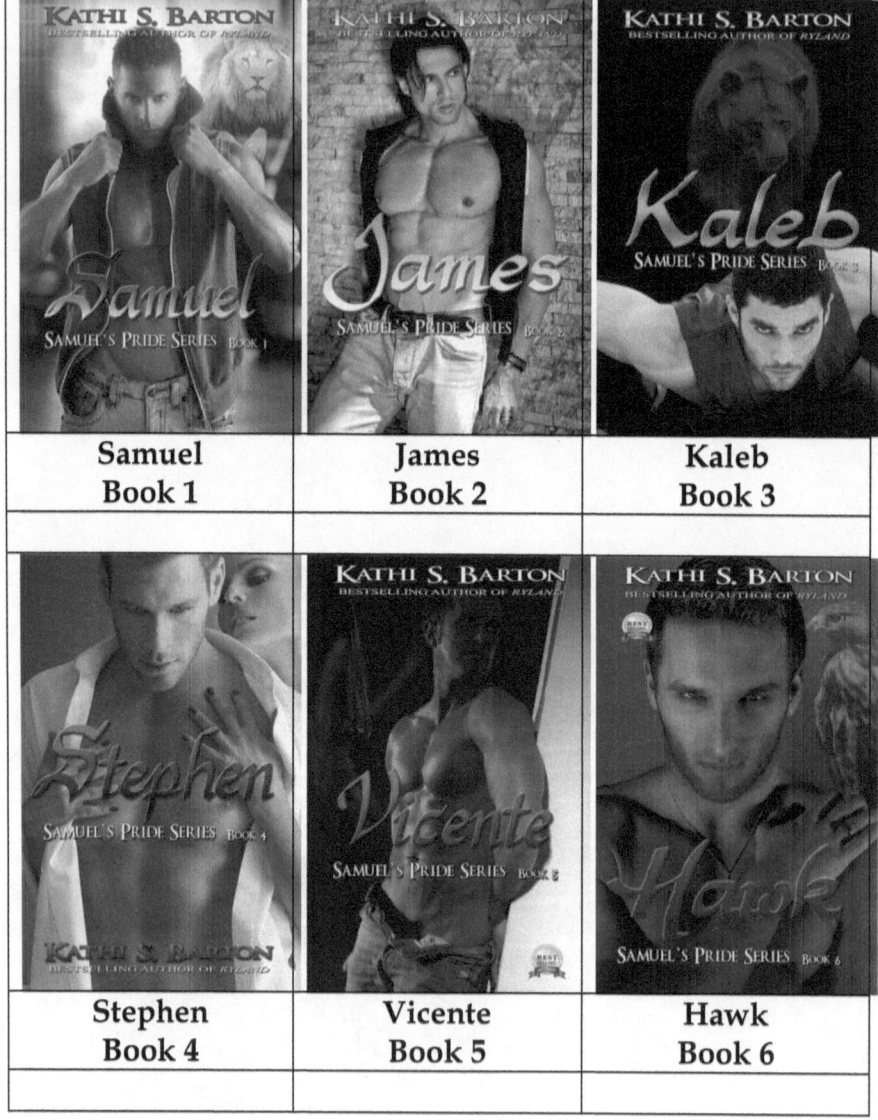

Samuel Book 1	James Book 2	Kaleb Book 3
Stephen Book 4	Vicente Book 5	Hawk Book 6

Before You Go...

Share your voice and help guide other readers to these wonderful books. Even if it's only a line or two your reviews help readers discover the author's books so they can continue creating stories that you'll love. Login to your favorite retailer and leave a review. Thank you.

AWARD WINNING, BESTSELLING AUTHOR

Kathi Barton, author of the bestselling series Force of Nature, lives in Nashport, Ohio with her husband Paul. In addition to writing full time Kathi likes to spend time with her eight grandkids, three children and three children-in-laws. She writes to relax and have fun.

Her muse, a cross between Jimmy Stewart and Hugh Jackman brings them to life for her readers in a way that has them coming back time and again for more. Her favorite genre is paranormal romance with a great deal of spice. You can visit Kathi on line and drop her an email if you'd like. She loves hearing from her fans. aaronskiss@gmail.com.

Follow Kathi on her blog: http://kathisbartonauthor.blogspot.com/